DESTINY
OF THE WITCH

BY HEATHER G. HARRIS

PUBLISHED BY HELLHOUND PRESS LIMITED

HELLHOUND
PRESS

Foreword

If you'd like to hear the latest gossip, bargains and new releases from Heather, then please join Heather's VIP newsletter.

You can sign up here, and as a welcome gift you get some *free* books.

Please also check out Heather's online store where she sells glorious merchandise and audiobooks. There are more hoodies, t-shirts, candles and stickers than you can shake a stick at. Delve into Heather's store at https://shop.heathergharris.com/

Content Warnings

Please see the full content warnings on Heather's website if you are concerned about triggers.

Please note that all of Heather's works are written in British English with British phrases, spellings and grammar being utilised throughout. If you think you have found a typo, please do let Heather know at heathergharrisauthor @gmail.com. Thank you.

For my awesome supporters on Patreon, with special mention to Amanda Peterman, Melissa and Kassandra. I am so grateful and humbled by your belief in me.
Huge thanks as always, to my amazing ARC teams! I am so grateful for all you do to help me!

Chapter 1

High Priestess Liyana was playing games.

Benji, Bastion and I were cooling our heels in reception. We'd had an appointment for 3pm and it was now closer to 3.30. I was sorely tempted to leave and find another seer – any other seer – but if I stormed off Liyana would ensure that no one else would see me. That was the sort of thing I'd done in the past and I was a little ashamed of that behaviour now. I would wait Liyana out; surely I had more patience than she had rudeness?

As time dragged on, however, my impatience boiled over into anger. She was being disrespectful, not just to me but to the Coven Council over which I now – somehow – presided. That disrespect could not stand.

Nell, the seer's receptionist, kept giving me furtive looks as if she were waiting for me to explode. That was enough to make me rein in my temper, so I was entirely level-headed when I instructed Bastion to kick down the door.

Nell squeaked as Bastion used his combat boots against the flimsy wood. The door banged open and slammed against the wall. We strode in, Bastion taking point, then me, with Benji bringing up the rear. Oscar was in the car ready for a quick getaway – which we might well need to make after the door debacle.

Liyana looked up coolly from her desk. She was hip-deep in paperwork and I knew how that felt, but nothing excused such disgraceful tardiness. People make appointments for a reason; if you can't keep to them, you shouldn't offer them.

I narrowed my eyes. 'Do you intend to sever all ties with the Coven Council?' I asked calmly.

She looked slightly taken aback. 'You don't have the power to—'

'I do,' I interrupted firmly. 'I am the Crone. Let me tell you what will happen if the witches withdraw their services from you. Your homes, your offices, public spaces – none of them would be runed. The vampyrs could slide into your offices and public spaces and kill you where you stood.'

I saw shock cross her face but she regrouped quickly. 'And how is that different to what happened to Melva?' Liyana snarled.

'Melva removed the protective wards on purpose in order to meet with the vampyrs. She didn't get them re-activated after the meeting.'

'If you're implying she is somehow at fault for her own death, I—'

'Of course not!' I snarled back. 'She was a victim. And if you hadn't left me cooling my heels for more than half an hour, you'd already know that I came here to tell you that her killer has been found and dealt with.'

She slumped back and gripped the arms of her chair. 'Taken to the Connection?' she asked tightly.

'No. This was a witch matter and it has been dealt with internally.'

'The necromancer,' she spat. 'Who was it?'

I hated having to admit it. 'A witch from my Coven. Jeb.'

Her eyes narrowed. 'I want him handed over to me for punishment.'

'That is not possible,' I said firmly.

She raised her voice. 'I demand—'

'Demand all you want.' I made my voice louder than hers. 'He is dead and his body has been burned. There is nothing left to give you.'

'He's dead?' Her hands gripped the edge of her desk in a white-knuckled grip.

'As dead as a Norwegian Blue parrot,' I confirmed drily.

A ghost of a smile rippled across Liyana's face before she got it under control. Evidently she was familiar with *Monty Python*, which made me like her a little more.

'Okay.' She rubbed a hand across her eyes and grimaced. I could tell that the next words were going to be difficult for her to say. 'I'm sorry that I kept you waiting.'

'You could have had this news half an hour ago,' I pointed out huffily.

She closed her eyes and nodded. 'I appreciate that you attended the office in person to let me know. It will be a great comfort to Melva's nearest and dearest to learn that she has been avenged.'

Now I was here, I needed two favours from Liyana. I battled with myself, but in the end I asked for the most important first in case she only gave me one. 'Good. To thank me, you can test these potions. Which of the four will work to cure an illness that resulted from temporal displacement?'

I pulled out four vials and laid them on her desk. I wasn't even entertaining the possibility that one of them might not work.

Liyana pressed her lips together but nodded sharply. 'Fine.'

She pulled out a crystal ball and a white bone dish, then poured a little of the first vial into the receptacle and gazed into the depths of the crystal. A moment later she blinked, cleaned the white dish and began again. She did it twice more until all four potions had been tested.

I knew in my gut which one would work.

'This one.' She pointed to the potion that held the claw clippings, hair and blood. I knew it – Indy had known what she was doing. Young as she was, she was already very smart. The potion needed more than a single ingredient from the hellhound to work. All three were needed to unlock the portal to the Third realm.

Liyana continued, 'All of the potions are safe for consumption, but this is the only one that will have the effect you seek.'

'Thank you.' I pocketed the correct vial and shoved the three remaining ones into my tote. You can't trust anyone other than a witch to do a proper potion disposal.

Liyana cleared her throat a little. 'Crone.'

'Yes?'

'It won't work,' she warned softly.

'What?'

'The potion. It won't work for your mother.'

'You just said—'

'I said that the potion will work to cure temporal displacement.'

'That's what I need.'

'Is it?' she asked pointedly.

'Yes,' I said firmly. 'So thank you.' My tone wasn't oozing gratitude.

'Thank you for finding Melva's killer so quickly,' Liyana stated.

'You're welcome. While you're feeling grateful, I have another favour to ask.' I might as well strike while the iron was hot.

'Another?' She arched an elegant eyebrow.

I ignored that. 'The enchanted cloaks you supply—'

She held up her hand to stop me. 'There are no records,' she said firmly. 'None. It is not the case that I *can't* or *won't* give them to you, but that they simply don't exist. There have been times in our history where we have been hounded for proof that X bought Y. These days we simply don't keep records so we have nothing to give, not an email address, a telephone number – nothing.'

'That seems imprudent.'

'Not at all,' Liyana replied. 'If we don't hold information, we can't be forced to part with it. All of our transactions are anonymous. The seer that made Bastion's cloak for your little excursion didn't know for whom she was making it. They never do.'

I refused to give up; there had to be *some* sort of trail we could follow. 'So how are orders placed?'

'Commercial ones are made through this office. Requests and payment are sent by post.' Before I could ask for any postmarks stamped on the envelopes, she stopped me. 'All the envelopes are destroyed after payment is verified.'

Sometimes the seers were more than a little annoying. 'You must have an address, to send the cloak,' I argued.

'Once payment is verified, the cloak is sent to one of our many safety deposit boxes. Before the initial request is destroyed, we send a communication to the address it came from confirming the box's location and giving a pin code to access it. When we've sent that, we destroy the request together with anything related to it, including which safety deposit box was used for delivery. We work through the safety boxes on a rolling schedule. The system guarantees anonymity. Deliberately so.'

'You're aiding evil witches.'

She shrugged. 'The perception of evil varies depending on which side you're on.'

'You're wrong. Torturing people – *killing* people – for magical gain is always evil,' I argued.

'What they do with the cloaks is none of my business. If we didn't sell them, another seer would.'

Things had started rocky, gotten smoother and now were back to rocky again. I was glaring at her with all my might, but before I could say something truly bitchy Liyana spoke again. 'If that is all, I have another appointment waiting.'

Apparently she didn't want to leave her next appointment cooling their heels. Not that I was bitter.

'And Amber?' she added.

'Yes?'

'I apologise if our working relationship has started on the wrong foot. Melva meant a great deal to me.'

I nodded and stood up. At the door I paused. 'I cared about her, too.'

I wasn't even surprised when the words felt true.

Chapter 2

Nell had recovered her aplomb. 'It is incredibly rude to kick in a door. I know you won't understand that because clearly you have no manners. Quite honestly, as the Crone, you are setting incredibly low standards, and yet—' she said primly '—somehow you're still failing to achieve them.'

That zing made me smile a little. 'Whereas you have delusions of adequacy,' I shot back.

She snorted. 'Bastion follows you everywhere, but only out of morbid curiosity.'

I grinned at Bastion. 'Is that it?'

'No,' he responded smoothly. 'It's the hypnotic swish of your skirts.'

I laughed aloud.

Benji frowned at Nell. 'You are being very rude to the Crone.'

'It's okay, Benji,' Bastion said. 'They are rude to each other because they like each other.'

Benji looked at us both aghast. 'What?'

'Nell and Amber are both uncomfortable showing affection,' Bastion explained. 'So they do it by exchanging thinly veiled insults that they both enjoy.'

Benji sighed. 'I fear I will never understand the human condition.'

'That's okay,' Bastion reassured him. 'Neither do they.'

Nell sniggered. I gave her a finger wave and a smile as we ducked out of the building to where Oscar was waiting.

We slid into the car. 'Everything okay?' he asked.

'We have a winner!' I said triumphantly.

'It took a while.'

'Liyana was playing silly buggers.'

'I hope you put her in her place.'

'Bastion kicked the door down.' Benji was almost bouncing on his seat. 'It was brilliant. I can't wait to kick a door down.'

'You've pulled a ceiling down,' I pointed out. 'That's even better.'

'It wasn't as dramatic, though. They do lots of door kicking in the movies. One day I'd like to do it, too.'

'You can do it next time,' Bastion promised with an indulgent smile.

Benji beamed. 'Thanks!'

Benji had control of the radio so we listened to some classic rock on the way to Mum's current house. He nodded his head in time to the music; he was turning into a proper headbanger.

When we arrived, Charlize smiled as she opened the door. 'Hello, lady and gentlemen, come on in. Luna is painting in the conservatory.'

We trooped in. As she'd said, Mum was at her easel. She looked frailer today, and my heart gave a painful twist. It had been too long since I'd last visited. Oscar was right: hard as it was when she didn't know me, I should still have come. Even so, it cut deeply as her gaze passed over us without a hint of recognition, not for me, not for Oscar, not for Bastion.

My stomach lurched. She was getting worse, so much worse. Why had her condition deteriorated so sharply?

I pulled out the vial but hesitated. Quite rightly, she wouldn't take medication from a stranger. Charlize saw the thoughts dance across my face and grimaced in sympathy. 'Pass it to me,' she murmured. 'I'll give it to her.'

I handed her the vial. 'Luna,' she said as she approached my mum. 'I have a new medicine for you.' She unstoppered the vial and passed it over.

Without comment, Mum drank the contents down in one. I hated that some petty part of me was jealous of Charlize; it didn't matter who Mum trusted to deliver her medicine as long as she trusted *someone*. All that mattered was that she didn't feel alone and scared. I wouldn't ever wish her to feel that, even if it felt a little like Charlize had replaced me.

I had suffered solitude for so much of my life, but what Mum was going through was so much worse. Losing your faculties must be so hard to bear. If she was comfortable with Charlize, that was a *good* thing.

I smiled hopefully and braced myself for some visible effect, some sign that the potion had worked. A minute passed. Two. Nothing.

Gutting disappointment wrenched through me and the smile slid off my face. The potion had done what it was supposed to do – healed temporal displacement. Liyana had confirmed that it would. Yet it had no effect on Mum at all.

Confused, I looked at Oscar and saw the resignation in his eyes. 'Dad?' I said softly. He turned to me. 'It hasn't worked, has it?' My voice caught.

He shook his head. 'No, kid, it hasn't. I'm sorry.'

I knew he was doubly sorry: sorry it hadn't worked, and sorry that he couldn't tell me why it hadn't.

I just wanted my mum back. I closed my eyes and tried to shove the heartbreak down. *It wasn't just about me*, I told myself firmly. Without Mum's help, I couldn't get into the encrypted CD any time soon. Without the CD, I couldn't learn what Mum had known about my father and how she had kept him from coming after us for all this time. I couldn't hunt down the leader of the evil witches. To do that, I needed the code to the damned CD, and the code was locked in her brain.

I consoled myself with the knowledge that Bastion had a hacker friend who would no doubt be back from his mysterious business soon, then we'd get into the CD one way or another. If I was honest with myself, what I'd wanted more than anything was to bring my mother back to me, to see her look at me and *see* me. Her blank eyes crushed me.

Hot tears rose but I blinked them away. I searched her frail face for something – anything. Just one hint, one micromovement to show that she was still in there.

But there was nothing. I looked into Mum's unseeing eyes and despaired.

Chapter 3

When I saw the incoming call from Dick Symes, I was almost relieved. It was hard to sit there seeing the polite smile on Mum's face that she reserved for strangers. I excused myself and went into the hall to take the call.

'DeLea,' I answered brusquely as I stared at the painting that hung in the hallway. I would recognise Mum's brushstrokes anywhere. She'd been here a matter of days, yet already she'd made this new house her home. She may be down, but she's not out.

'It's time for favour two.' Dick got right to the point.

'What do you need?'

'Some truth runes. Bring the griffin.' He hung up.

I despised being summoned like I was a lackey. Dick might not be aware of my promotion yet, but I was now one of the most important witches in British society and being summoned like an acolyte set my teeth on edge.

Chapter 4

Dick insisted on total privacy, so of course Frogmatch scurried into his house to create havoc. I watched with a faint frown as his forked tail disappeared through an open window. 'I'm beginning to think I have no control over his actions.'

Bastion grinned. 'What was your first clue?'

I sighed. Benji and Oscar were far more obedient and happily stayed in the car. They were listening to some classic rock and Oscar was teaching Benji to play air guitar. Their burgeoning friendship was as unlikely as my friendship with Benji, but no less beautiful. Oscar didn't have many friends; as my guard and enforcer, he had to stay at arm's length from most of my Coven. For all he was a wizard, everyone knew that he had my ear.

The stress of the visit with Mum was still visible on his face, but the tension started to loosen in his shoulders as he talked animatedly with Benji and a smile crept in. I was beginning to realise that friendship is one of life's greatest treasures; I'd been a fool to avoid it for so long.

I was about to knock on Dick's door when my phone rang. I didn't recognise the number but I swiped to answer the call. 'DeLea.'

'Amber!'

I instantly recognised Jinx's exuberant tone and the dark shadow over my heart lifted a little. 'Jinx, how are you?'

'I'm good,' she answered warmly. 'How are you?'

I opened my mouth and imagined telling her all about the evil Coven and Abigay and my ascension to Crone-hood. Then I closed it again. She was on her *honeymoon;* she deserved to relax for once.

Mindful of her truth-seeking abilities, which extended to talking to people over electronic devices, I cleared my throat and said, 'I'm okay. Things have been turbulent, but there have been some really positive developments.'

'Any positive developments with Bastion?' Her voice was lightly teasing.

'Yes. We've had sex,' I blurted out. Next to me Bastion's shoulders started to shake with silent laughter.

'Oh, Amber, I'm so happy for you! I mean ... this is good sex, not angry sex, right? You've come through your differences?'

'Yes, good sex. Great sex.' I felt my cheeks redden and cut myself off before I used the word 'phenomenal'. Bastion's ego was big enough already. Amongst other things.

I realised I'd better tell her about removing the curse from him. It felt like a lifetime ago, but it had only been a matter of weeks. 'I've lifted the witch's curse from him,' I said.

'Oh, thank God. Thank you, Amber!' Her relief was explosive and I felt another prickle on my conscience. Bastion was like an adopted uncle to her and she really cared about him. Though not in the way I did, that was for sure.

'There's more to tell you,' I said gruffly, thinking of Jake. 'But maybe not over the phone.'

'Sure, I have stuff to tell you, too. We're heading back in the next few days. Let's have a coffee, a blueberry muffin and a catch-up when I'm home,' she suggested enthusiastically.

I smiled. 'I'd love that.'

'Good. Amber?'

'Yes?'

'This is me, calling just to say hi. I haven't had my phone on me for most of my holiday – we're trying to stay unplugged as much as possible – but I've been thinking of you.'

'Thanks, Jinx. I appreciate that.' I was about to hang up when Bastion held out his hand. I passed him my phone.

'Jessica Sharp,' he greeted her. 'Emory is looking after you?' I didn't hear her response but Bastion smiled. 'Good. See you when you're home.' He hung up.

'You didn't even say goodbye!' I said, exasperated. 'You have terrible phone manners.'

He smirked. 'I don't want to burst your bubble but I have terrible everything manners. You're the only one I say please and thank you to.'

I didn't know what it said about me that I felt a little surge of desire at that. His smile widened: he'd felt it.

The front door was flung open and Dick glowered at us. 'If you're quite done lolling about on my doorstep, get in!'

Bastion's head shifted in a purely eagle movement and his eyes flashed gold as he glared back. Dick retreated, swallowed hard and suddenly looked a little less certain of himself. 'Please,' he added lamely.

I kept the grin off my face with herculean effort.

We walked into the water elemental's home, not to his lounge as I'd expected but down some stairs to a wine cellar. It was cool and dimly lit, and the tinkle of a water fountain added to the damp, dark ambience. As a water elemental, Dick could call forth his element from nothing but it was a lot easier to pull water from nearby a source such as the fountain.

In the centre of the room was a man tied to a chair. He was soaking wet and shivering, but his eyes were defiant. I grimaced. Walking into a scenario like this always made me feel like the bad guy. I tried to not let that show; displaying your morals in the Other realm is like showing a wolf your jugular – highly inadvisable.

'Who have we got here?' I asked coolly, gesturing to the bound man. I didn't recognise him.

'Miles Turner,' Dick replied just as coolly. 'It seems he is part of a mercenary band of elemental renegades that call themselves Unity. There are four of them.'

'There were four of usI'd thought,' Miles glared at me, 'until you killed Keith.'

I hadn't killed many men in my life, but one was still unnamed: the fire elemental I'd killed when he'd attacked me. 'Fire elemental?' I asked, raising an eyebrow.

Miles pressed his lips together, refusing to speak further. Now, that was a problem. I could paint truth runes on him until the potion boiled, but if he didn't speak all we'd get was a whole lot of truthful silence. A truth-seeker like Jinx could compel him to speak but I didn't have that weapon in my arsenal.

That, however, was Dick's problem, not mine. I opened my bag, snapped on my gloves and opened the jar of truth potion. At the sight of it, Miles started to thrash violently and tug against his restraints. He was going to ruin my runes if he did that while I painted them on.

'Stay still,' I said sharply. 'If you make me bungle the runes, the effects could be deadly.' I wasn't even lying.

He stilled. Sensible man. I painted a large truth rune on his forehead, then ran my magic through to activate it.

'You can go,' Dick grunted.

'I don't think so,' I said primly. 'This is *my* rune work and I want to ask him about the fire elemental.' I didn't want to call the fire elemental by his name because it felt too personal; it made him a man rather than a deadly enemy that I had been forced to smite. The nightmares already bothered me; I didn't need to make it worse.

Dick frowned. 'That wasn't part of the deal.'

I drew myself up to my full height and levelled a look at him that would have made most grown men pee their pants. 'I am the Crone. I will question this man or I will end my rune work here and now and you can forget your damned favour.'

He blanched. 'Crone? I hadn't heard.' He gave me a little bow. 'Of course, you go ahead, Crone.'

I didn't bother to acknowledge his sudden fawning but turned instead to Miles. 'As part of your group, you have an earth elemental. Yes?'

He glared at me.

'Bastion, rip a finger off for every question he doesn't answer,' I instructed calmly. 'When we run out of fingers, we can use toes.' I really hoped the threat would be enough, because Bastion wouldn't have any issue with pulling off body parts if it got me the results I wanted. I really didn't want to be responsible for Miles' maiming – though I supposed I could heal him after Bastion's mutilation so he wouldn't be harmed long term.

I grimaced. It would be okay, as long as I didn't use Miles' pain to bolster my magic. Therein lay the dark side. Morals all squared off, I met his gaze and let him know I meant business.

He blanched. 'They'll kill me if I talk,' he said finally.

'We'll kill you if you don't,' Bastion growled. 'You're between a rock and a hard place, but the difference is that I'm here right now.' For emphasis, he shifted his hands into claws.

Miles paled.

'So,' I started again. 'Earth elemental... Yes?'

'Yes.'

'Name?'

'Gareth Clark.'

'He attacked my mum?' I demanded.

Miles licked his lips before nodding.

'And who is the air elemental in your little group?'

'Simon Morris.'

'Excellent. And who hired you all to attack me and my mum?'

'The black Coven.'

'And you have no issue with that?'

'No. We're *mercenaries*.' He sneered at me, as if I were an idiot for not understanding what that meant.

'Even mercenaries can have a moral code,' I snapped back.

He smirked. 'Not us. We'll do any job if the price is right.'

'Lovely,' I said drily. I was feeling better about my annihilation of the aforementioned Keith. If this group had no moral code, who knew how many lives they'd already destroyed? 'Who was your contact at the Coven?' I asked.

He opened his mouth to talk, then abruptly black threads started to spider out from his eyes. The threads continued to grow at a speed faster than I'd ever seen before. He started to convulse; it looked like black mordis poisoning on steroids.

'Get him out of the ropes!' I ordered Bastion hastily as I wrenched open my tote and looked for the stasis potion. I found it, grabbed a fresh paintbrush and dunked it in the jar.

'Get his shirt off!' I barked. Bastion cut away Miles's shirt and I started to paint frantically: *isa*, *algiz* and *sowilo*.

Miles was being poisoned. I had Whole Remedy with me, which would heal eighty percent of poisonings – but not black mordis. Still, it was worth a shot if I could stabilise him first – this wasn't black mordis so maybe Whole Remedy would work. I painted runes as fast as I could.

He was convulsing violently and starting to foam at the mouth. Despite my efforts, he had one last seizure and I knew instantly that I couldn't save him.

'He's gone,' Bastion said a moment later.

I dropped the paintbrush on the cellar floor and clenched my teeth. 'That's not just black mordis,' I said finally. 'That happened way too fast, faster even than it did for our girl.' I didn't name Ria because Dick was listening.

I tidied up after myself and tried to keep my face calm, but inwardly I was raging. The evil Coven's reach was terrifyingly far. I had no idea how they had killed Miles from a distance. An embedded curse that activated under a specific set of circumstances seemed likely, but that was incredibly complex rune work. I could think of only five witches in the whole of the UK who could do something like that.

Either way, Miles was dead and Dick didn't look too pissed off with the outcome. 'Why aren't you more annoyed?' I snapped.

He grinned. 'The water elemental part of Unity is dead so officially Unity is no longer my problem. I'll deal with the body. Thanks for the favour – it turned out even better than I'd hoped.'

What a complete donkey-butt. I hoped Frogmatch had wreaked havoc on his home. At the very least, I hoped the imp had swapped his salt and sugar round and tied his shoelaces in elaborate knots.

I'd love to screw with Dick further, but quite frankly nature had already handled that.

Chapter 5

I dreamt that night of the fire elemental, Keith. Of a fireball ploughing towards my head whilst I frantically tapped my watch to slow time to give me a few precious seconds to duck. In my dream, the watch didn't work and Bastion wasn't there. The fireball hit me and I burned, my skin cracking and peeling whilst the flames consumed me. Keith stood over me and laughed, shouting, 'Burn bitch!'

In the distance, my mum watched and did nothing.

I awoke with a choking sob. Bastion's arms were already around me and he stroked my hair, whispering a constant litany of love and reassurance. I shook in his arms as I sobbed my heart out. If anyone else had been there I would have tried to throttle back the tears, but as it was just Bastion I let myself go.

A repetitive tap on my bedroom window finally pulled me out of my crying jag. I knew that tap. 'Let him in?' I asked Bastion softly.

He kissed my forehead and padded across the bedroom, naked and unselfconscious. When he opened the window and Fehu flew in, I felt the jet-black bird's concern like a tingle on my skin. 'I'm okay,' I reassured him. 'It was just a bad dream. A really horrible one,' I conceded, 'but a dream nonetheless.'

'Kraa!' he said firmly. He flew to me but didn't land on my naked shoulder; instead he landed on the duvet covers and hopped anxiously from foot to foot.

I smiled. 'I really am okay, Fehu.' I reached out and stroked his feathers. 'I'm sorry I upset you. It was only a dream.'

'Tell us about it?' Bastion asked softly.

'It was about the fire elemental. You didn't get to me in time and I burned,' I said, keeping my tone as matter of fact as I could manage.

'I'm sorry.'

I snorted. 'For what? In real life, you *did* get to me in time. Clearly my subconscious is feeling bad about Keith's death. It's harder, now that I know his name – it makes him human, a man that lived and breathed and had a mother and a father, and probably someone that loved him. And I killed him.'

'He attacked you. You defended yourself. He was a mercenary – he knew the risks of every job he took,' Bastion pointed out. 'He knew witches carried potion bombs and yet he chose to attack you. His death is on him – and maybe his employer – but definitely not on you.'

'A little bit on me, Bastion,' I said with a wobbly smile. 'I threw the bomb that killed him.' Admittedly, I hadn't intended to hit him, but my aim was terrible.

'If he'd walked on by, he would have lived. You can't choose other people's paths, only your own. Let it go, Bambi.' He kissed my forehead again lightly. 'Do you want to try and go back to sleep?'

I checked the time: 3am. I winced, but all hints of sleepiness had faded. 'No, I'm not going to get back to sleep now but you go ahead. I'll get up and do some more potion work.'

'I'll work out, then we can have breakfast together,' he suggested instead.

I smiled gratefully. 'Sounds perfect.'

I slid into the shower and washed the nightmare's sweat off me. I dried and dressed perfunctorily, runed myself up, then sat on my dresser chair and looked into the mirror to make my affirmations.

'I am grateful I saw Mum yesterday. I am grateful I have Bastion in my life. I am grateful for all the challenges that I face because life is never boring. Today, I am going to create a potion to save Lucille.'

I nodded at myself, at the determination in my face. The first step in achieving anything is self-belief – and I believed in myself in spades.

Time to save Lucille.

I poured over the DeLea potion bible. There wasn't anything in there that could help Lucille directly, but I made notes about a few potions I thought I could combine.

I'd started work last night before exhaustion had pulled me under. Despite the nightmare, I felt fresh and my brain was clear. My main problem was that I didn't know what was ailing Mum, and Mum and Lucille were intimately and permanently connected. I'd been so sure it was temporal displacement, but the potion hadn't worked – not because it wasn't right but because the issue with Mum was something else entirely. Without knowing exactly what was wrong with her, it would be difficult to fix.

Lucille's problem was that she was giving too much of her energy to keep Mum going. I needed to give her both a physical and a magical energy boost until I could get to the root of the problem and help Mum.

My ORAL potion gave a magical boost, but it didn't have a physical energy component. I was pretty sure I could add to it, but potion interactions are tricky. I pored over my old textbooks, checking for mention of any adverse reactions with kelpie waters. Unfortunately there was none – because no one had survived the kelpies long enough to borrow their waters. That put me slap-bang in unknown territory. Luckily, the unknown doesn't faze me.

My best bet was to combine the energising and the ORAL potions, but I'd have to remove certain elements from the energising potion that would react badly, then I needed to substitute other ingredients to reflect the reductions. I would definitely need to remove corydalis, but I was confident I could bring in velvet bean and griffonia without any adverse effects. Motherwort, of course, to strengthen Lucille's heart. I had neither of those in my personal store, but the Coven store was sure to have them.

I reviewed the potion that I'd been researching to help Kass with her fibromyalgia. I could take the rhodiola, which is used for chronic exhaustion, from it. Confidence surged through me as I realised I had a very good starting point; I just needed to work out what amount of each ingredient needed to be added, and that was a matter of gut instinct rather than science.

I frequently measure with my soul rather than my weighing scales; that is my true gift in potion excellence. Something – instinct or the Goddess Herself, perhaps – tells me exactly the right amount of each ingredient as I brew. It is the one thing I've never managed to impart when I teach. I can teach the acolytes how to follow a potion recipe, but to make them into potion masters is something else. It is a calling, not simply a job.

I dashed down to the potion store with Bastion on my heels. I'd walked into the bedroom while he was in the middle of his workout and a fine sheen of sweat covered his body, but he'd pulled on a T-shirt and insisted on coming with me. I tried hard not to get distracted as I looked at him and shoved the ingredients I needed into my bag. I signed them out and gave Briony a smile as I left.

I jogged back up the stairs to my apartment; that counted as fitting in some exercise. When we walked in, Bastion shucked his shirt off again and started to do crunches. I left him to it and hauled my spoils back to my lab.

I cleaned the surfaces and decided to get started: there's no moment like the one you are in. First I brewed a fresh base in my pewter cauldron, making notes as I went so I could replicate the potion exactly. That way I wouldn't need to listen so closely to my gut when I made it next time, and it would be on hand to teach to others if it proved efficacious.

For now, though, I tuned into my instincts: a little more motherwort, less lemon balm, make the potion hotter… When I was satisfied that it was ready, I added the final ingredient, Lucille's blood, to maximise the potion's efficacy. It would bind the potion specifically to her.

I stirred it in and the cauldron shone golden. I grinned in exultation.

Finally, the potion was ready for cooling, decanting and testing. Optimism buzzed through me, a welcome lift from all the negativity I'd been struggling with. This was going to help Lucille, I was sure of it.

Chapter 6

Bastion looked up as I walked in. 'Success?' he asked.

I grinned. 'Yes, I think so. It needs to be tested, but I'll get one of the acolytes to run it by Liyana or another of her seers if she's not available.'

'Hopefully this time, she'll fit you in,' he groused.

'She will. I think we have an understanding.' I hoped so, anyway.

'I've made breakfast, but it's more like brunch now.'

I checked the time: 11am! Whoops. I'd gotten lost in the potion. My stomach let out a growl.

'Better feed the beast,' Bastion teased. 'Sit down. I'll warm it through and bring it over.'

He had cooked us a full English breakfast. I often struggled to eat first thing in the morning, but luckily we were far past that. I attacked the food with gusto, thankful that he'd even done hash browns. When I'd finished, I pushed the empty plate away. 'That was amazing. Thank you.'

'You're welcome.'

'Now probably isn't the right time to raise this, but I thought that I probably need to learn a little more hand-to-hand combat if we're going after some evil witches. At the moment it feels like they hold all the power.'

'Amber,' Bastion looked amused, 'the other day you ripped the Earth in two to get rid of some zombie ogres. Believe me, you have power aplenty.'

That made me smile a little.

'Having said that,' he went on, 'there's no reason why I can't teach you a few tips and tricks to make you feel more confident.' He pushed back from the table and grabbed a pillow. 'Why don't you show me how you'd kick this?'

I stood, lifted my skirts out of the way and then – without understanding what I was doing – did a roundhouse kick that sent the pillow flying out of his hands. Bastion's mouth dropped open.

I blinked. 'Huh.' I toyed with the pendant at my neck. Edith – one of my Crone predecessors – had known how to kick butt. She'd taken over my body to save me with a spot of knife fighting and it seemed I'd also inherited some of her other skills.

'That was unexpected,' Bastion noted.

'You remember when Tristan attacked me?'

'How could I forget?' he growled.

'He had a knife. I asked my sisters if anyone could help me. A lovely witch called Edith took over, kicked his ass and shoved him into the pentagram.' I paused. 'Then you ran in and killed him. But it looks like some of Edith's skills have been left behind.'

'Whether you have her skills or not, you still need to practise. You won't be comfortable using them if they're not embedded in your own body and mind,' Bastion counselled.

I nodded reluctantly. I'm not a huge fan of exercise, and I have the cardiac fitness of a cursed slug. But things were heating up and I was determined not to be the weak link. He was absolutely right. It was something to work on.

'Ok, I'm game if you are.'

'Always.'

Bastion held up the cushion. 'Again.'

Our impromptu training session had felt surprisingly good. My arms ached a little with all of the punches that Bastion had made me throw, but I was pleased at how far I'd come on. Goddess bless Edith. It helped that I was probably the first young Crone to be appointed in recent years, and that was another advantage I had. I was physically, and magically, still at the height of my power – if I trained right, I could be a force to be reckoned with. A prophecy hung over me, and I was all too conscious that I really needed to be a force to be reckoned with.

'Thank you for my training.' I kissed him. 'And thank you for the brunch too.'

'You're welcome. What are your plans for the rest of the day?'

'I need to speak to Ethan and do some general Coven-keeping. Now I've been awarded the role of Crone, we need to start the process of finding a new Coven Mother.'

I got out my laptop and fired off a few emails, then summoned an acolyte to take Lucille's potion for testing.

I was surprised – and impressed – when Sarah Bellington was the first to volunteer.

Moments later she was at my door and hustling off to the seers, potion vial in hand. It had seemed mean at the time but demoting her to acolyte because of her poor crystal ball safety had clearly been the impetus she'd needed to push herself. I gave myself a mental pat on the back for my excellent leadership skills.

I sent a few more emails before Ethan knocked at the door. He and I weren't friends – or even friendly – but we had a decent working relationship that did the job. Though I always felt he was bristling to attention every time we spoke.

Bastion let him in and came to stand by my side; he was in guard mode and he let Ethan see it.

Ethan ignored any implicit threat and got straight down to business. 'The discovery of a black witch—'

'Evil witch,' I corrected.

He went on without missing a beat. 'A necromancer no less, in our Coven! Well, it's going to cause issues.'

I raised an eyebrow. 'For whom?'

'For all of us,' he huffed. 'As if it isn't bad enough being known as the Hula Coven,' he muttered, pacing in front of my sofa.

'The salt rings are sensible,' I started to argue.

He raised a hand. 'I have no issue with the practice, just the disrespectful nickname.'

I smiled. 'You know how we deal with disrespect.' A curse a day keeps the idiots away.

A smile flickered across his stony visage. 'Well, yes.'

'Then let them be disrespectful. They'll only do it once.'

Ethan sat on the edge of the sofa. 'Jeb,' he said tightly. 'I still can't believe it. We've worked together for years. I feel like I can't trust my own judgement.'

I knew exactly what he meant. 'We can't let them undermine us. Jeb acted a part for years. It's not our fault for taking him at face value.'

'I don't know where we go from here.'

'We do exactly what we were doing before,' I said firmly. 'We keep an eye on our potions store, and we keep an eye on practising witches. We know their power levels. Jeb was a mid-level witch when he came here, but when he broke an old clearing in my mind there was absolutely zero sign of exertion. With hindsight, that was a huge red flag that I missed. We need to review the personnel files, check their initial tests. Perhaps we could redo some power tests as part of a Coven shake-up. If anyone's power has increased unusually, we'll know to look at them twice.'

I didn't share with him the recent survey that the Coven Council had carried out while the evil witches were off in the daemon realm. I had a number of names on my list to look twice at.

Jeb had been on there, but Venice Bellington was also on the list and it would truly be a surprise if she were evil. Melrose was also there, and I was disquieted to see Hannah on it too because she was one of my protégées. If Hannah's excellence came through pain and death rather than natural talent and hard work, I'd be sorely disappointed.

Ethan's name wasn't on the list, but the fewer people who knew about its existence, the better so I wasn't planning to mention it. I had suggested strongly to the Coven Council that the list be for the Coven Mothers' eyes only, and only after someone had checked that the Coven Mothers themselves weren't on it. That sort of snafu was something that happened all the time in big organisations, and it was as embarrassing as it was dangerous.

'That's a good idea,' Ethan said, relaxing now that he had something he could do.

My phone blared. I intended to ignore it but I checked the screen just in case. *Abel calling*. My gut clenched. Abel was the pseudonym that I used for Cain Stilwell's number.

The ringmaster of the Other Circus didn't call me for casual chats.

'Excuse me,' I muttered hastily to Ethan. 'I need to take this.' I strode into my office for some much-needed privacy and swiped the screen to answer.

Chapter 7

'You need to come to the circus,' Cain said urgently. 'There's been an incident.'

'What's happened?' I asked, my voice tight.

'Meredith has been attacked.' He paused, picking his words carefully. 'They intended for her to die but we got to her in time. She'll be okay, thank God. But she's not safe here any longer.'

He sounded upset. I got that; he was running a safe haven that was no longer safe. A safe haven I helped to fund and run.

The Other Circus exists solely to give any of the magical population a place to hide if they are on the Connection's radar, or if they've fallen foul of a powerful person from the Other. A select few seers and witches help direct people to the circus when they have need of it, like I had directed Meredith and Ria. Meredith should have been safe under

Cain's roof, but she wasn't – and now everyone else in the circus was in danger too. Someone's enemy knew where and what they were. Worse, it was *my* enemy. The circus and its occupants were in danger and it was my fault.

I closed my eyes and rubbed my forehead. 'I'm sorry that I brought danger to our door.'

'We're all running from danger here, one way or another. We're always prepared for it to come knocking,' he said grimly.

Cain had been a werewolf alpha and a proponent of equal werewolf rights. Someone hadn't liked the cut of his jib; after multiple attempts on his life, he had faked his own death and gone into hiding in the circus before he could be silenced permanently. After a few years, Cain had taken over running it. He was a born leader. Though he may have been prepared for his enemies to find him, the circus had always been a safe place. Until now.

'But danger hasn't knocked before,' I argued guiltily. 'Not like this.'

He snorted. 'Amber, take that chip off your shoulder. We've had plenty of incidents over the years. I may have glossed over them with you, but you know about the one a few months ago when one of our runaway centaurs was found by his abusive father. We dealt with it.' The father

DESTINY OF THE WITCH

had been dispatched – permanently. 'And we'll deal with this. But come now. Ria needs you,' he said firmly. 'And so do I.' He hung up.

Exasperated, I redialled. He answered the phone but didn't speak. I sighed. 'How am I supposed to know where to come?' I huffed. 'Where are you?' It was a *roving* circus.

'Ah,' he made a sheepish sound. 'Liverpool. The Liverpool Arena.'

'I'll be two or three hours,' I promised. 'I'm on my way.'

He hung up again. Terrible phone manners, but I forgave him because he was stressed.

I went back into my lounge to make my excuses to Ethan but found that he'd already left. I guessed he wasn't in the mood to await my pleasure. Bastion raised an eyebrow in question. He hadn't followed me into the office, so he probably hadn't heard the contents of the call even with his supernaturally sharp hearing.

Melva had said that I would have to tell Bastion about the circus soon and it looked like she was right. Even now, I hated that a little. I hate anyone predicting the future – especially mine.

I cleared my throat. 'Have I told you the secret about the circus?'

'What secret?' Bastion asked lightly. 'That there's a trick to all of the clowns getting out of the same car?'

'Not that.' A smile pulled at my lips despite my anxiety.

'There *is* a trick to it,' he said in all seriousness. 'There's a trapdoor underneath the car.'

I hit him lightly on his muscular arm. 'Not *that* secret. I run a circus.'

He blinked. 'I can honestly say I didn't expect that.'

'It's an undercover circus,' I explained. 'Everyone there is Other, but they live and exist in the Common realm, hidden from their enemies and – or – the Connection. A few witches and seers know about it and help direct people in danger there. The ringmaster either settles them into circus life or helps them start a Common life somewhere while they're moving up and down the country. There are whole pockets of hidden Other-realm communities content to stay away from magic if it means they keep their lives. That's where I hid Ria and Meredith. At the circus.'

His expression cleared. 'And now?'

I sighed, my shoulders tight with stress and tension. Worry for Meredith coiled in my gut. Worry, and guilt. I'd promised that she'd be safe at the circus. 'And now the evil witches have found them. So we're off to the Liverpool Arena.'

He stood. '10-4. I'll get the others on standby. Can you pack your bags and be ready to move out in five?'

I loved it when Bastion used military lingo – and he knew it. I suspected he was trying to distract me from that little kick of guilt he'd no doubt felt through our bond. That made my heart melt a little too. Damn, but the man was the complete package: considerate and sexy. None of that showed on my face, however, and I nodded calmly. 'I'll just grab some of the rarer healing potions. Cain didn't specify what I'd be dealing with, only that Meredith had been attacked but was still alive.'

As I went to pass him, he thrust out an arm and caught me around the waist. I squeaked as he pulled me close. 'Bastion! We're in a hurry!' I protested. I could read the intention in his eyes, and the intention was salacious.

His eyes were dark. 'There's always time for us, Bambi.' He leaned down and kissed me like we might never get another moment alone together. His lips were firm and unyielding, and his tongue slid into my mouth like he was conquering me. In seconds he had fanned a wisp of desire into a full-blown roar.

When he pulled back, his eyes were satisfied. 'Much better,' he purred. 'Go pack. We'll finish this later.'

I tried to get my synapses to fire but he'd short-circuited them. There had been a time when I'd thought nothing and nobody could boss me around, not even my baser instincts. How things had changed. It turned out I was quite happy for my primal urges to rule me sometimes.

'Healing potions,' Bastion prompted with a smug smile, pushing me towards the fridge.

Right. Meredith. Healing potions. I consider myself an intelligent, cerebral woman, so it still amazed me that Bastion somehow knew how to shut down my overthinking brain and connect to my more improper impulses. Impulses I'd never really had a chance to explore properly. But now was not the time to dig into them.

Meredith, I reminded myself and kicked my bum into gear. I grabbed a bunch of healing potions, including some Whole Remedy, the leftover brain swelling potion and an incredibly strong burn salve. I didn't know what ailed Meredith, so I had to be prepared for as many eventualities as possible.

It was time to save Meredith. And then it was time to find whoever had harmed her and make them regret it for the few fleeting seconds of life that Bastion allowed them before he put an end to them. Permanently.

Chapt

I knew the Other circus almost as well as I knew my own Coven tower. Every month I painted complex warding runes into each caravan, which meant that over the years I'd frequently met the occupants.

For most of them, I was their sole connection to the Other realm, a way to get news and gossip about what was happening in the magical world that they'd forsaken. I was a bit of a celebrity, which wasn't a feeling I enjoyed. I'm not a gossipmonger, though I tried to dredge some up for the circus occupants. Sometimes they needed – and deserved – a slice of normal life.

The previous month I'd let Hannah Lions accompany me to the circus to help with the warding, and now Meredith had been attacked. That, together with Hannah's name being on the Coven Council's list, put Hannah slap bang at the top of my suspects' list. The thought feel rather ill. Hannah was hard working and conscientious, and I saw a lot of myself in her. But maybe hard work was too much and she'd taken shortcuts. Maybe blood work had turned to pain work, and pain work had turned her to the dark side. Maybe she was an evil witch.

I hated the thought but it buzzed loudly in my brain for the whole journey. I even logged onto the Coven systems to check where she was. It noted her as having an allotted day off yesterday and today.

Witches don't work a Monday to Friday week. We have a rolling schedule that ensures we have coverage twenty-four hours a day, seven days a week. The attack had fallen on Hannah's two days off. A smart evil witch would have done it on her working days and manufactured some fake jobs to give a concrete alibi. Perhaps Hannah wasn't as smart as I thought, or maybe she really wasn't evil.

Though my brain was stuck on the latter, I would not ignore the facts because I didn't like them. In life we all have to face facts that challenge our beliefs, and I was determined not to be wilfully ignorant. But dammit, I really didn't want Hannah to be the culprit.

I strode confidently towards Cain's black caravan; it was top of the line, his one indulgence as ringmaster. That was where he would help anyone who was injured or upset, so no doubt I would find Meredith there.

Stu caught sight of me. 'Amber's here!' he yelled loudly. He looked behind me and blanched when he saw Bastion and Benji on my heels, then gaped as he caught sight of Frogmatch riding shotgun on the golem's shoulder. Oscar stayed in the car, protecting the vehicle from tampering and ensuring we could make a quick getaway should one be needed. 'She's brought allies!' he called.

'Yes, thank you, Stu,' I chastened. 'No need to announce the colour of my knickers as well.'

He blushed. 'Sorry, Miss Amber. We've been worried. Mere is in a bad way.'

I quickened my pace then launched myself up the caravan steps, knocked once and let myself in. Ria looked up as I entered. Her blue eyes were red-rimmed and her flaxen hair was loose around her shoulders in total disarray as if she couldn't stop carding her fingers through it. She was sitting next to Cain and his arm was tucked around her.

Cain's face was lightly lined and he had a sprinkle of silver in his dark hair, but he was still devastatingly handsome. His eyes were tired but he still held himself with purpose.

'Clark,' Bastion said in surprise.

Clark Farrier – now known as Cain Stilwell – gave Bastion a small nod. 'Bastion. I trust I can rely on your discretion, not just about my death but about the whole circus.'

'Yes, of course. I give you my word that no one will learn of it from me.'

'Meredith?' I interrupted impatiently.

'We found her hanging,' Cain said grimly. 'We cut her down as quickly as we could and resuscitated her. Although she's breathing on her own now, she hasn't come round.'

Ria let out a soft choking noise and her familiar, a mouse named Fido, nuzzled into her neck.

The hospital was out as an option for Meredith. Hospitals have crossover staff, people that work both as doctors *and* healers. Cain couldn't risk the paperwork that might end up sliding across the Connection's desk. It was me or Common medicine grabbed from a pharmacy, and the latter would be wholly inadequate. Without magical intervention, Meredith would need to be carefully monitored in a hospital, particularly for brain damage.

'In your bedroom?' I asked briskly, already moving that way.

'Yes,' Cain confirmed.

I opened the door and went in with Bastion on my heels. Meredith's hair was spread out on the pillow like a pale halo. Her face was ashen and the skin around her throat was already darkening with bruises. Her brain had been deprived of oxygen for Goddess knew how long.

Luckily, I had brewed a brain-swelling potion for Oscar not long before, the main treatment for cerebral oedema and hypoxic brain damage. Despite its short shelf life, it would still do the trick for Meredith. The small amount of innate magic she had in the Common realm would be enough to spark the potion into working. Thank goodness I'd had it to hand; it was rare for me to brew it let alone carry it with me. I gave thanks that Oscar had been struck on the head when the fire elemental had attacked me; it would probably save Meredith's life.

I opened my bag and pulled out the yellow vial. Bastion carefully searched the room; once he had ascertained that it was safe, he stepped out to speak with Cain. He left the door ajar so that he could hear if I needed him.

I opened Meredith's mouth and poured a little of the yellow potion into it. As I had with Oscar, I closed her mouth and stroked her throat so that she swallowed reflexively. Unlike Oscar, she did exactly that. I repeated the process until the vial was empty.

Her eyes fluttered and she awoke with a strangled gasp. She shot upright, hands moving to her throat, eyes wide in panic.

'You're okay,' I assured. 'You're safe.'

'Mother!' she croaked in relief when she saw me. She fell into my arms and started to sob.

I patted her awkwardly. 'Everything's okay. You're safe now,' I repeated.

The door pushed open. 'Mum!' When Ria ran in, Meredith left the comfort of my arms and instead offered comfort to her daughter.

'I'm okay.' She smiled bravely through her tears, then wiped at them, not wanting her daughter to see her cry. Her voice was hoarse and croaky; there was no doubt she was in pain from the damage her neck had endured.

I opened my tote bag, found potions for muscle damage and bruises and pulled out a small paintbrush. 'Let's heal that throat.'

Ria moved off her mother's lap so I had some more space to work in, but she clung fiercely to Meredith's hand. 'Ouch!' Meredith murmured. 'I still have bones in that hand,' she joked. 'I'm glad to see you too, baby.'

Ria snorted. 'I'm not a baby.'

'You'll always be my baby,' Meredith replied, kissing her lightly.

Meredith had always been well-groomed, so it was odd to see her now with her hair wild, face naked of makeup and nails with the remains of last month's manicure half-grown out and picked at. She'd been through some truly difficult times, and I suspected that they weren't over yet.

I painted on *hagalaz* for injury and *sowilo* for health, first using the muscle damage potion then the one for bruises. I examined her with a critical eye then painted on two more runes for good measure. The more runes you use, the more of *your* magic you use to activate them, but even so I have never been one to skimp on magic. Results matter.

I drew my magic forward and traced it through the runes. They lit up and I watched with satisfaction as the bruises faded before they could get truly established.

Meredith smiled at me. 'Thank you, Coven Mother. That is so much better.' She touched her neck self-consciously.

'No problem. I'm glad you're okay.'

I studied her. Her colour was up and she looked steadier. Her tears had stopped when her daughter arrived. 'Good,' I said abruptly. 'I have some questions for you.'

Meredith's smile faded. 'No doubt.'

'Did you see your attacker?'

Meredith looked down and away as she squeezed her daughter's fingers. 'No,' she said softly. 'I'm sorry.'

I shook my head. 'Whatever they said to you, I need to know the truth.'

'They didn't say anything. I didn't see anyone,' Meredith insisted. I wasn't sure I believed her, but now wasn't the time to press while her fear was still so strong.

'They wrote a message. In blood,' Ria said tremulously. 'They wrote, "There's no quitting the black Coven, Ria. You can't hide from us. We're coming for you next". We're not safe here, Coven Mother. We need to go home.'

I narrowed my eyes. They could damned well try and get my witches but Ria was under my protection now, and I would keep her safe through any means necessary.

Chapter 9

From the moment I'd met Frogmatch, Bastion had treated him with respect. I hadn't understood why until the little imp had grown to gargantuan proportions and started to tear through the evil Coven with his antlers. He had vowed to protect me – but right now I needed him to protect someone else.

'A word?' I asked the imp.

He swung down off Benji's shoulder, scuttled across the floor and climbed me like I was a jungle gym. 'What can I do for you, Crone?' The respect with which he spoke took me by surprise. He was so jovial most of the time that it was rare to hear a serious tone in his voice. I realised that I'd often underestimated him and I made a mental note to stop that; there was nothing humorous about the imp when he wanted to be deadly.

'I need you to guard Ria and Meredith. I need them safe. I'll ask Charlize if Meredith and Ria can join my mum. Even though she is guarded by rune wards and griffins, more occupants means that additional guards will be needed. I saw what you can do. Will you help keep Ria safe for me?'

He puffed out his chest. 'Aye, I'll keep her safe,' he vowed.

'Thank you.' I touched my hand to my chest to show him how much I appreciated his agreement, and his little chest swelled again with pride. He swung down from me and skittered over to Ria and Meredith.

'This is Frogmatch,' I introduced him to the witches. 'He's my—' indentured servant? '—loyal friend. He will keep an eye on you both, keep you safe.'

Ria frowned, no doubt thinking that he wouldn't be much help at all. I didn't elaborate on Frogmatch's skillset; that was for him to disclose as and when he wanted to. Most species prefer to keep their skills hidden; that's one of the reasons the Other realm is so dangerous. Even to its experienced, knowledgeable occupants, it is still a riddle wrapped in a mystery inside an enigma. Woe betide the fools who think they know all there is to know about the Other realm.

I excused myself and went to speak to Cain. Bastion and he were talking in low voices. 'Sorry to interrupt,' I said, though I didn't sound especially sorry, nor did I feel it. We needed to get things in motion and I was feeling impatient. 'We're going to take Meredith and Ria with us. We'll see them secured somewhere else. Hopefully that means the evil Coven won't have any interest in the circus after that.'

Cain grimaced. 'I hate the idea that I've failed them, but you're right. Much as it pains me to admit it, they're not safe here.'

'Exactly,' I agreed briskly. 'I need to check the wards. Someone came in here and attacked Meredith. Even though she can't – or won't – tell us anything about her assailant, we know she was attacked on site during the night. That means the wards were interfered with.'

'So her attacker was almost certainly a witch,' Cain said sombrely.

'And a male one,' Bastion noted. 'They struck her over the head first and then hoisted her up. They had to be strong to do that.'

'Or they weren't working alone,' I pointed out.

'Or that,' he agreed.

I rifled through my tote bag and pulled out the protection potion for ward runing. It wasn't quite as effective as using blood in the protection wards, but not by much.

I untacked the poster on the inside of the caravan door and touched the runes with my magic. Though they lit up promptly, the glow was soft like a firefly's. I scanned them but they were in perfect working order, though the reduced glow showed that they were weakening. Another runing would be required in the next week or so. I sighed inwardly; I might as well do it while I was here.

'Bastion,' I called over my shoulder, 'I'm going to re-rune the circus while we're here. Can you rip away these protection wards? It'll save me one job. Then I'll re-do them.'

Bastion nodded. His eyes glowed golden for a moment and the wards in front of me melted like snow in the desert. 'Thanks,' I muttered and started painting.

This time, as well as the normal protective runes, I added a little defensive bite. It took more time, more effort and more magic, but if another evil witch came strolling around there'd be a sting in the tail if they tried to cancel the runes.

It wasn't black magic – but it was decidedly grey. I found that I didn't care too much; if someone came prowling around to deactivate protection wards, they only had one purpose in mind. I painted more protective runes so my scorpion runes would be hidden at first glance. If the witch was in a hurry or just lazy, my runes would bite them in the ass.

Once Cain's place was done, I moved determinedly onto the next caravan. In the thirteenth, I found where the runes had been cancelled and the witch had slipped in. The warding runes worked together in harmony, keeping the entire circus safe. A misalignment or a cancellation introduced a weak point that someone could exploit.

After painting protective runes on fifty caravans, I was running on empty and my skin was itching like mad. I didn't have any of my ORAL potion to hand. I resisted the urge to scratch; it isn't dignified to scratch at yourself like a dog with fleas.

I texted Charlize and told her that we would be bringing two more people in for her to protect.

'It feels horrendous,' Bastion said in a low voice to me.

'What?'

'The itch. I never appreciated how horrible it is. I thought you humans were just exaggerating, but it's almost unbearable. And I'm only feeling it second-hand through our bond. I don't know how you're not mauling your skin.'

'Through sheer stubbornness,' I admitted.

A smile ghosted across his face. 'That sounds like you.'

Bastion came from the creature side of the Other divide, so he never had to go back and forth through portals and his magic never waned. It was surprisingly gratifying to have him acknowledge what human magic users went through.

'You get used to it,' I said.

'It's enough to make you want to rip your skin off.'

'Hopefully Oscar has some ORAL potion in the car. If not, we'll have to stop at a portal.' I didn't really want to do that, not with Ria and Meredith in my care and under my protection. A portal is always a point of weakness no matter what security the elementals offer, and it always feels vulnerable.

I went to say goodbye to Cain. He was talking to Victoria Dubois, the circus's fortune teller and they were leaning close. There was a familiarity there that told me they were more than friends. Victoria was a beautiful young woman; Cain was incredibly attractive too and they made a stunning pair. If they had been famous, they would have had some sort of mangled joint name like Brangelina – Vain perhaps. I snickered to myself.

Victoria was as powerful as she was beautiful. She was an incredibly gifted seer; even stuck in the Common realm as she was, she could still see glimpses of the future. When she was younger, many people had expected her to become High Priestess one day but then she'd disappeared. I hadn't asked her why she'd needed to hide because that is an unwritten rule in the circus: no one talks about *before*. It's too raw to consider all you have lost.

'We're all done here,' I said firmly to Cain. 'I've runed you all to the hilt. You'll be absolutely fine.'

'Thank you, Amber.' Cain looked relieved and the tension eased from his shoulders.

'A word, Crone,' Victoria said.

'Crone?' Cain was taken aback. 'You've had quite the promotion. I didn't think you were old enough for the role.' His voice was a little sharp.

I winced. I probably should have mentioned the new title and all that went with it, but my focus had been on Meredith. 'A recent promotion,' I muttered a shade defensively.

'A word – alone,' Victoria repeated.

I turned to Bastion. 'Can you get Meredith and Ria settled in the car? I'll sit in the back with them, Benji in the front. You'll have to fly, I'm afraid.'

Bastion shook his head. 'No, you ride with me and they can take the car. We'll meet them at our final destination.'

I opened my mouth to object then closed it. I didn't *want* to be separated from Bastion; the last time that had happened, I'd ended up in a dank jail cell. 'Fine. Can you see if Oscar has any ORAL on hand?'

Bastion moved away and Cain also stood up and left me alone with the seer.

'What did you need to talk to me about that needs privacy?' I asked bluntly.

Victoria looked grim. 'We need to speak of your future. What else, Crone? The Goddess tells me I must read you.'

I pursed my lips; I despised talking about my future as if it were immutable, but who was I to deny the Goddess? I folded my arms and waited for Victoria's pronouncement of my fate. 'Well? Go on,' I waved at her impatiently.

'A touch would help me achieve a clearer read,' she suggested.

I didn't want a clearer read, but I did want this whole conversation to be over and done with so I held out my hand imperiously. She grasped it and her eyes glowed. By the Goddess, she was powerful if she could access her powers to that extent even in Common.

She let out a strangled gasp before dropping my fingers. The light faded from her eyes and she looked at me with sadness in her eyes. 'I don't have enough power here to pull a true prophecy for you, but what I saw will come to pass. I'm sorry, Crone.'

'What?' I asked evenly. 'What did you see?'

'Your mother's death, at your own hand.'

'Never!' I gasped.

'You plunged a blade into her heart – but it will save us all.'

I shook my head and stumbled back from her. Never. I would *never* harm Mum. For all I cared, the world could burn before I did that.

Chapter 10

Bastion touched my wrist lightly. 'What's up? You're upset.'

'Not here,' I murmured desperately. 'We need to go. Let's just go.' There was an edge of panic to my voice that I knew Bastion could hear and feel. I struggled to put my emotions into a box inside of me. I couldn't lose it here. Victoria was *wrong*. That's all there was to it.

The others were in the car, waiting for Bastion to shift into griffin form for me to ride with him. My phone rang. I was going to ignore it, but then I saw who was calling: Sarah Bellington. Now that was something I could cling on to. I needed some good news. Surely the potion I'd made for Lucille would work, and that would be one thing I could do to help Mum – not kill her.

I swiped to answer. 'Tell me good news,' I demanded.

'Yes, Coven Mother,' she responded happily. 'The potion works. It will help an ill familiar gain magical strength!'

I sagged a little. 'Great,' I said briskly, letting none of my relief show in my voice. 'Get back to the Coven. And Sarah?'

'Yes?'

'Good work.' I hung up and turned to Bastion. 'You heard that?'

He nodded and gave a small smile. 'You're a genius. Was there any doubt that your potion would work?'

I loved his faith in me. 'Yes,' I said drily. 'There was doubt.'

'Not in my mind,' he reassured me. He pulled me close and kissed my forehead tenderly. 'You're all wrung out, Bambi. You need to rest.'

He wasn't wrong but I shook my head. 'We need to get the potion to Lucille because I'm not sure how long she's got. We don't have a moment to waste.'

'I'll compromise,' Bastion offered. 'We'll fly home, have dinner, then we'll take the vial to Lucille. Then it's back home and straight to bed for you.'

I thought of his hot kiss and whispered promise earlier. 'Only if you join me.'

'Always.' Bastion fished out a small vial from his pocket and held it out to me: ORAL potion. I had never been happier to see one of my own potions.

I unstoppered it, downed it in one and the vile itching receded instantly. 'Thank the Goddess,' I murmured with a sigh of relief.

'Thank *you*,' Bastion corrected lightly. 'The ORAL potion is all down to you and your hard work.' He passed me the harness from his black backpack and then he shifted. I laid the harness on the ground, he stepped in, and I buckled it around him.

I didn't bother saying goodbye. Cain and Victoria were talking intently and I didn't want to disturb them, and it may have been petty but I really didn't want to talk to Victoria right then. She clearly thought I was someone I wasn't. I might deal with the monsters but I wasn't one of them – though the line between us felt more and more blurred every day. The scorpions I'd just buried in the circus wards were testament to that.

I climbed onto Bastion's back, hooked my feet in the stirrups and gave him a light pat that told him I was ready. I looked at the car: Oscar was watching me go with an unreadable expression, and Ria was laughing as Frogmatch played with her familiar, Fido. He was rocking the sleepy mouse in his arms like a baby.

I gave Oscar a thumbs-up and he nodded. He started the engine, which was our cue. I felt Bastion's muscles bunch and tense and then he exploded forwards. When we were moving fast enough, his wings snapped out and with two mighty beats we were airborne. I watched as the car got smaller and smaller.

It felt a little like my conscience.

Chapter 11

Bastion and I flew right into a storm, and the rain pelted me and the wind whipped at me. He struggled valiantly to lift us above the clouds, but they were thick and heavy. It felt like forever before we burst above them.

'Thank the Goddess,' I called out, though the gusts stole the words as soon as they left my mouth. I hunkered down low on Bastion's back, letting his body and wings offer some protection from the elements. Though we were out of the rain, the wind still blew fiercely around us and I was soaked to the bone. I started to shiver uncontrollably.

Luckily Bastion's speed meant that we weren't far from the Coven tower. I was looking forward to getting home. Bastion's suggestion that we eat before we went to see Lucille was a great one, but I also added having a steaming hot shower to my to-do list.

Finally he dived. I recognised the tower's roof right away, and he landed feather soft on top of it. He barely waited until I'd climbed off before shifting into human form and pulling me into his warm body. It felt decidedly unfair that his body was virtually an inferno whilst I was a shivering, quivering wreck.

'Sorry,' he murmured. 'Shitty weather.'

'You're not kidding.'

Night had fallen and the stars winked at me. Being on the roof beneath them suddenly transported me back to another night weeks earlier, when Abigay's eyes had turned milky white as she'd gazed at the stars for me.

My mouth dropped open. As the Crone, surely I could do the same? What need did I have for Victoria's horrible prediction? I could see my own! 'I could read the stars!' I blurted.

Bastion shook his head firmly. 'The only thing you're reading tonight is a romance novel. You're wiped out, Amber, and you're shaking with cold. Let's get you warm and fed, then we'll visit your mum and Lucille. Hopefully Oscar and the car will have arrived by then.'

'Griffin Air is faster.'

He grimaced. 'But colder. I should have checked the weather before insisting you come with me. I should have just flown above the car.'

'If the Connection knew you were flying so close to cars where Common realmers could spot you, you'd be in trouble,' I argued.

He shook his head. 'The Other realm protects itself; you know that. All the Common realmers would see is a giant eagle.'

'Maybe – but the Connection still wouldn't be happy.'

He raised an eyebrow. 'Since when have you cared about the Connection?'

'I wanted to be the Symposium member once,' I said primly, pushing away from him. 'For a long time I wanted to work within it.' And now I'd be outside of it forever because the Crone couldn't be a Symposium member.

It was strange to realise that letting go of that dream still stung a little. The Connection was a good organisation in theory, but in practice too many bigots held positions of power. It was corrupt, lumbering and slow, not the unifying organisation that we needed it to be. For a long time, I'd wanted to be the one to revolutionise it, to bring about the change it needed, and letting go of that ambition was bittersweet. But my role as Crone would bring different challenges and different rewards.

Maybe Kass could introduce the changes that we needed. A good leader delegates, so this task would be all hers. And if I was a little jealous? For me, that was personal growth.

Bastion felt the swirl of uncomfortable emotions within me and tugged me to his side. He kissed me lightly. 'Let's get inside.'

The warmth and wards of the Coven tower wrapped around me as we entered. I was so eager to get to my apartment that I all but jogged down the stairs. Bastion keyed in the code on the security pad on my door and let us in. He immediately headed to the kettle – a man after my own heart.

'Get out of those wet clothes,' he ordered, 'and I'll run you a hot bath.'

That was an even better idea than a shower! 'Deal! I'll make us a cup of tea.' While the kettle boiled I went into the bathroom and pulled off my wet clothes, cringing as the wet fabric dragged against my skin. I dragged on a fluffy dressing gown, almost sighing with relief as its soft fabric rubbed against me. I was still feeling glacially cold but things had certainly improved.

I went back to the kitchen to select my mug. I pulled out one that said *Today I'm going to be more useless than the 'G' in lasagne* because it felt true. I was wiped out and, I could admit to myself, a bit low. A lot low. Meredith had almost been killed on my watch. Victoria thought that I could and *should* kill my own mother. Someone had subverted my protective runes on the circus. I was working so hard, yet nothing was going my way. I felt like Destiny had me in her crosshairs.

I wanted to confront Hannah, but an interrogation was the last thing I could handle right now. Besides, I still needed to give Lucille her potion. If Lucille died... I couldn't even finish the thought. Saving her was about all I had left in me. Tomorrow I'd confront Hannah – but after at least six hours sleep.

My tummy rumbled so I made a quick slice of toast while my tea was brewing. Bastion's mug said *You are the human equivalent of a participation trophy.* It made me laugh because it couldn't be more inaccurate. He was a specimen of male perfection and he knew it; as his girlfriend or partner or whatever I was, I needed to keep his ego in check. Just a smidge. He already knew he was glorious.

'Bath's ready!' he called and I went into the bathroom, mugs of tea in hand.

He had put in masses of bubbles that towered above the bath like a gargantuan white castle. I was momentarily speechless. 'I think I overdid the bubbles,' he said, a shade sheepishly.

I wanted to assure him that he hadn't but I burst out laughing instead. 'Oh, Bastion,' I finally managed to say while I still giggled. 'How much did you put in?'

'All of it,' he admitted. That set me off again.

When I finally stopped laughing, I slid out of the robe and got into the bath. The water was hot perfection and I gave a happy noise. The chill in my limbs would be gone in no time. I hummed contentedly.

When I was submerged, I could hardly see Bastion for the cloud of bubbles. That made me start giggling again. He stepped forward, gathered an armful of them and plonked them on my toes so at least I could actually see. 'Better?' he asked.

'Perfect,' I smiled. 'Don't change a thing.'

'Well, one thing,' he said. 'Give me a minute.' He disappeared from the bathroom and I took the opportunity to grab my mug and sip my tea, warming me from the inside out. I had an inkling about what might be coming; after all, there is nothing better than reading in the bath.

Bastion came back in and held out a book. I grinned as I read the title: *The Bite Side of Life.* The blurb told me it was an enemies-to-lovers romance about a monster hunter and dashing millionaire vampire.

'I've noticed that all the books you give me are enemies-to-lovers romances.'

He winked. 'I had to plant the seed somehow.'

'Sneaky griffin.' I tried to act as if I was telling him off, but he could feel the amusement behind my tone.

He kissed my forehead. 'Read and relax while I make us food. Oscar texted that they'd just stopped for a toilet break. They're still an hour away, so we have time.'

I was finally feeling warm now, but it had nothing to do with the heat of the bath. As Bastion went to draw back, I used one hand to give him a bubble beard. My peals of laughter followed him as he left the bathroom. There was no way on this green Earth that I'd got the drop on him, which meant that he'd let me bubble him up to make me smile.

My heart felt suspiciously, almost painfully, full. I had tried for as long as I could to avoid naming the feeling that burned through me, but now I couldn't deny it even to myself. I loved Bastion. Head-over-heels, gut-churning, I-can't-wait-to-see-you love. He was my first thought every morning and my last thought every night. I cherished every moment I spent with him, even if we were standing over a dead body or facing a gang of zombie ogres together.

I loved him. Completely and utterly.

And I didn't have the first clue what to do about it.

Chapter 12

Bastion and I borrowed a Coven car to get to Mum's address, which he fastidiously checked over for bugs or transmitting devices. When he was sure we were all good, we drove off. I was behind the wheel for a change and Bastion was in the passenger seat, keeping an eagle eye out for any tails or any danger. I had about as much chance of spotting a tail as a first-week acolyte had of completing a batch of final defence. We each have our skills in life, and it's important to embrace them.

As we drove, I felt a familiar presence join us. I looked up and Fehu swooped down obligingly so I could spot him even against the inky night sky. I guessed Bastion had summoned aerial backup.

Luckily, backup wasn't needed and the drive was un-eventful. We stopped outside the safe house and parked behind Oscar's stationary vehicle. Bastion got out first, opening my door and covering me with his body as we hustled inside.

Charlize let us in with a warm smile. 'Hi, Dad, Amber. Come on in.'

The lounge was spacious but still a little packed with all of us in there. I worried that we might stress Mum, but one look at her standing next to Meredith set my mind at ease. She was talking animatedly, busy showing off her latest artwork. Mum and Meredith had once known each other quite well, and I could see that they were happy to see each other.

I looked hopefully at Oscar but he gave a slight shake of his head; Mum might know Meredith today, but she didn't know Oscar and probably wouldn't know me. I tried to shove down the bitterness.

Frogmatch was busy tying the laces of Ria's Converse boots into intricate knots, much to her amusement. Fido lounged on the toes of her shoe, watching with mild interest.

Benji rumbled over to me and gave me a cold hug. 'How was your flight?' he asked solicitously.

'Wet and cold,' I grumped. I didn't mention the bubble-bath thing; Bastion probably wouldn't want that sort of thing coming out and ruining his reputation. 'Have you seen Lucille?'

'She's next to Oscar.'

'Great. Can you find me a plate then meet me in the hallway?'

'Of course, Am Bam.' Benji headed to another room – the kitchen, hopefully.

I waited until Oscar met my eyes then pointed to Lucille and nodded to indicate he should bring Mum's familiar into the hallway. When he picked up her small body, I hated how frail she looked cradled in his arms. She used to be so full of gambolling energy, and it was just wrong to see her so motionless, so lifeless. My breath caught.

Bastion went to speak to Charlize and the other two griffins, Apollinaire and Haiku. Oscar and I went into the hall with Lucille. 'Lay her there,' I told Oscar, gesturing to the bottom stair.

He set her down carefully whilst I rooted around in my bag for the vial. When I found the right one, I opened it and carried it over to the limp ferret. 'Hey Lucille, I need you to drink this, okay?' She blinked sleepy eyes at me but gave a distinct nod.

Benji joined us, carrying a small side plate and a large dinner plate. 'I wasn't sure what size you needed.'

I smiled gratefully and took the smaller plate from him. 'Thanks, Benji.' I poured some of the potion onto it and set it down next to Lucille. Her small pink tongue poked out and lapped, slowly at first and then suddenly much faster as energy started to surge into her limbs.

I poured a little more until my gut said that would be enough for now. She lapped at it enthusiastically and, when the plate was clean, she gave a chittering laugh. She scampered rapidly around my feet before she flew under my skirt and tangled around my legs.

I laughed. 'It's good to see you're feeling a little better – but still no going under my clothes!' I said as I fished her out. She wriggled in my arms and leapt up to wrap herself around my neck. My smile felt like it would never fade. I stroked her little head and she batted against my fingers.

Happiness was bursting in my chest. I hadn't been too late! I might have failed Meredith, but I hadn't failed Lucille. And hey, Meredith was still alive, so I was chalking up today in the win column.

'Let's take you to see Mum,' I suggested to Lucille. 'She'll be so happy to see you've got your va-va-voom back.'

Sitting on my shoulders, she chittered excitedly. As I walked in with her, the room quietened. 'That's strange,'

Mum commented with a confused frown. 'Lucille doesn't usually like strangers.'

Her words hurt, but I tried hard not to show it and keep my face blank. 'I have a way with animals,' I said tightly.

Lucille knew how hard it was for me and she nuzzled me comfortingly. Then she leapt down from my shoulders and careened across the room to Mum.

'Lucille!' Mum laughed and clapped her hands with delight. 'Well, I can see you're feeling better! She's been a little under the weather lately.' Lucille ran up to where she was sitting, leapt on the sofa and ran circles around her.

Mum laughed again, and my happy glow was back. She was pleased, and that was all that mattered.

Chapter 13

Once we were sure that Ria and Meredith were settled, Oscar, Bastion, Benji and I made tracks. As Frogmatch watched us go from the window, he gave me a cheeky salute and a wink. I found that I was oddly comforted that he was there; I had no doubt he would give his all to keep the occupants safe.

I gave him a solemn salute, which made the smile slide off his face. He gave a deep bow then disappeared to protect my witches for me.

Bastion and I followed behind Oscar in the Coven car. We parked in the garage and started upstairs – until a loud noise from the common room made me veer off the steps.

There was a huge gathering. There was music, nibbles and drinks. There were bowls of crisps, sweets, a huge vat of jelly and a can of squirty cream. I raised an eyebrow at Ethan and he came across to join me.

'Things have been tense,' he offered as an abrupt greeting. 'They needed an opportunity to let their hair down – they deserve it. I sent out a Coven-wide email.'

I hadn't checked my email all day. A nagging part of me worried that I was letting the Coven down; I was so busy chasing evil witches that I hadn't taught a lesson in weeks, let alone checked on the potion store or authorised some holiday leave.

I looked around. I rarely enjoy parties: I'm a book and a hot drink kind of a girl, but we're not all the same.

I could see Henry sitting a little too closely to Sarah on the couch. He seemed to be getting over his 'true love' of Ria awfully fast now that she wasn't in the picture. Sarah was twirling her hair around her fingers and smiling flirtatiously at her best friend's boyfriend. I wanted to tell her that was a bad idea, one she'd regret, but it wasn't my place. At a certain point, you have to let the kids make their own mistakes. Teenage hormones are a terrible thing.

John and Venice were talking animatedly about potion ingredients. He was promising to show her a rare ingredient later and I cringed, hoping that wasn't a euphemism.

Briony, Timothy and Ellen, who I thought of as the 'lazy' witches, were in another corner. Melrose was talking to Ethan's husband, Jacob, and Hannah's guard, Edward.

Hannah herself was nowhere to be seen. That settled in my stomach like a stone, but I tried not to let it show on my face.

The music changed from pop to rock and I saw Benji grin and nod his head in time to the beat. 'If you like that,' Henry said, pulling his eyes off Sarah for a moment, 'I have some awesome tunes for you to listen to.'

Oscar and Benji exchanged a glance, and Oscar shrugged indulgently. They went and sat by the teens. Henry fished out some earbuds for Benji to listen to something on his phone.

John spotted me and came over. 'How are you, Coven Mother?'

'I'm fine thanks, John.'

'I heard from Sarah that you successfully created a potion for energising familiars. Is someone's familiar ill?'

Damn it. I hadn't told Sarah that the potion was to be kept on a need-to-know-basis. In my rush to help Lucille, it hadn't even occurred to me that the potion I'd created could also be used by evil witches to heal their sick familiars. Bloody hell: once again I'd painted a huge target on my back, and Sarah was out there telling everyone about it.

I pinched the bridge of my nose. 'I need to teach Sarah about discretion,' I said and sighed. I'd make sure to speak to her tomorrow.

'Don't be too hard on her. I noticed this morning that you'd logged out some velvet bean, motherwort and griffonia. I would have guessed you were making some sort of strengthening potion. But for whom?' he asked again.

I smiled and patted his arm lightly. 'That's on a need-to-know basis.' My tone was friendly but the insinuation that *he* didn't need to know was clear.

John nodded, his expression serious. 'No problem. I'll speak to Sarah about discretion, shall I?'

'Thanks, that would be great.' I removed it from my mental to-do list. 'John, before you go, have you seen Hannah lately?' I asked as casually as I could.

He frowned, 'Now that you mention it, no – I haven't see her for a couple of days.' His expression cleared. ' But I have been very busy at the Shoppe. A newspaper put us in a very complimentary article and we've been busy with Common realmers coming in.'

The Spice Shoppe helped fill the Coven's coffers. Though the majority of the profits were reserved for helping Covens in need, it was still positive news. 'That's great. Thanks.'

He gave me a smile and a slight bow, then made a beeline for Sarah. I watched, hiding my own smile as he frowned at her and gestured wildly. He even shook his finger a little. I watched as she shrank back. Hopefully she would remember to employ a little more discretion next time she was sent on a Coven task.

Part of me thought that I should stay and socialise with my witches, but having the boss there would dampen the party atmosphere. Besides, I had plans with Bastion. He may not remember them, but I certainly did.

I sidled towards the door and Bastion followed me with a faint smile. As we left, he reached out and snagged the can of squirty whipped cream.

Okay, maybe he remembered we had plans too.

Chapter 14

I awoke feeling energised and ready to kick ass. Today was going to be *my* day: I was going to confront Hannah about the circus and get some damned answers.

Bastion had laid a fresh blueberry muffin and a cappuccino on the dining-room table. I ate the breakfast of kings with gusto, while he devoured a veritable bucket of porridge. I guessed it took a lot of calories to keep that machine in top shape.

As I ate, I studied my apartment. All around there were little signs of Bastion's cohabitation: some free weights tucked in the corner of my living room, his favourite brand of coffee on my kitchen counter. He'd even put up the paintings that Mum had given us. I didn't know how to deal with the fact that, to all intents and purposes, he had moved in. I also couldn't help but hope that the arrangement would be permanent. What the heck would I do if

Bastion left for another job? Surely he was still at Shirdal's beck and call? My heart started to race at the thought of him leaving me. I'd grown so accustomed to his solid presence in my life. If he went back to other jobs, how would that affect us? I blew out a long breath and tried to shove the panic down. We'd work things out. We had to.

I was still thirsty after my cappuccino, so I checked in the fridge. I frowned when I saw no overnight oats or freshly squeezed orange juice. Perhaps Oscar had stayed at the party for too long and chugged too many beers but... A tendril of worry wormed its way into my gut. I texted him, asking if he was awake.

Whilst I was waiting for a response, I got out my laptop and checked the Coven roster. Hannah was due to work in the Coven's potion lab today but it was still only 7am, so she wouldn't be there yet. I bit my lip. It would probably be best to see her in her apartment: the fewer witnesses, the better. We'd catch her at home in 2C on the second floor before she went to the lab.

I checked my phone: still no response from Oscar. He was an early riser and I'd never known him to still be sleeping after 6am. Fear curled in my tummy.

Bastion walked out of the bathroom, a towel looped around his hips. 'What's the matter?' he asked, looking around sharply. 'You're worrying.'

'Oscar didn't leave me any orange juice.'

I was fully prepared for him to smirk at me or roll his eyes, but he did neither. Truth be told, he had never belittled my fears. 'I'll get dressed and we'll go to his apartment now,' was all he said.

I noted that he didn't tell me Oscar would be fine. Through our bond, I felt his own concern ratchet up. Damn. Now I was *really* worried.

While Bastion dressed, I grabbed a bunch of healing potions from the fridge and shoved everything I could think of into my tote. Bastion emerged moments later and we silently jogged down the stairs to Oscar's floor.

I knocked once on his door but neither he nor Benji answered. I pounded on the door but still no one came. Panic licked through me.

Bastion gently pushed me aside, put his boot to the lock and kicked it forcefully. His eyes glowed yellow, and he tore down the wards I'd carefully painted for Oscar only a couple of weeks ago. Normally I'd have objected to such a heavy-handed approach, but I was running down the roads of panic and brute force seemed just fine and dandy.

'Dad?' I shouted as I ran in.

I let out a strangled cry as I came upon Benji. He was frozen, turned into stone just as he had been about to stand up. His eyes were wide with panic, but his skin had no shine of life. To all intents and purposes, he looked like a statue. He'd been deactivated.

'Benji!' I gave a choked cry as I rushed to him. I touched his cold cheek but there wasn't an iota of magic or life in the cold hunk of clay in front of me. Fear welled up; I had managed to save him from deactivation once before, but that had been in Edinburgh, in the seat of power itself where the ley lines intersected.

'Amber!' Bastion called sharply from Oscar's bedroom and I ran in.

Oscar lay on the floor beside his bed, glowing with activated *isa* runes. His pyjama top was discarded next to him, and I could see a pen clenched in his fist. On his chest, his arms, even his legs where he'd rolled up his pyjama pants – every scrap of skin he'd been able to reach – he'd drawn on *isa*.

I felt his neck and sobbed when I felt a faint pulse. He'd done it! He'd managed to put himself in stasis in time. 'Poison!' I murmured darkly. 'He must have been poisoned and when he realised what was happening he put himself in stasis.'

'How?' Bastion frowned. 'He's a wizard.'

'You of all people should know that runes can be used by anyone – to a degree. Oscar's grandmother was a witch so he has some very minor latent skill. It was obviously enough to light up the runes, thank the Goddess.'

I tried to treat him like any other patient. I rolled him over so he was lying on his back and examined him critically. No spidery black veins, so it wasn't black mordis. His lips weren't purple, so it wasn't 8987. I checked his lungs: no sign of collapse so it wasn't Veldrake's Revenge. Relief shot through me. Most poisons could be nullified by a number of antidotes and I had a couple with me. If neither of those worked, I would brew the others.

I grabbed the vial of Whole Remedy. It contained activated charcoal, atropine and sodium bicarbonate, with comfrey leaf acting as the stabiliser, and it would save about eighty percent of poison victims. I prayed it would work for whatever ailed Oscar.

I held my breath as I pried open his mouth and carefully poured in a small amount of the remedy, then rubbed his throat to make him swallow reflexively. This time he did so. I repeated the process until the vial was empty.

I felt his pulse: it seemed stronger. I waited with bated breath, studying his eyes. When they snapped open, I felt a surge of relief. 'Help me get these *isas* off him,' I said to Bastion. I took a bag of baby wipes from my bag and started to scrub at Oscar's skin. When half of them were removed, the stasis broke.

'Benji?' he asked urgently.

I shook my head. 'I don't know. It looks like he's been deactivated again. I've never heard of a golem surviving multiple deactivations, but we have to try. What happened?'

'Someone poisoned me!' Oscar spluttered, outraged.

'Any idea who?' I asked.

He grimaced. 'By the end of the night we were all sitting in a big circle. I'd drunk four or five beers.'

I took out a small flashlight and flashed it into his eyes. His pupils shrank in response. I held his wrist and counted his pulse.

'Did you drink out of a bottle, a can or a glass?' Bastion asked.

'Bottle.'

'Did you unscrew the caps yourself?'

Oscar frowned. 'Not all of them. At the end of the night, someone gave out all the remaining bottles.'

'Who?' Bastion barked.

'Edward, I think – and Jacob.'

'This is all very nice,' I interrupted, letting Oscar's wrist fall. 'But now that Oscar isn't in danger, we need to focus on saving Benji! We can find the culprits later.'

Bastion studied me. 'I have never heard of anyone reviving a golem.'

'That doesn't mean it *can't* be done. I've done it once before, I can do it again.' I refused to entertain any other possibility. I would *not* lose Benji. I stood up. 'I need to go to my apartment. Can you two check on everyone else who was there last night?'

I held out another vial of Whole Remedy to Oscar and he took it.

Bastion shook his head. 'I'm not leaving your side.'

'Time is of the essence,' I argued. 'If anyone else has been poisoned like Oscar, we need to find them now.'

'Time *is* of the essence,' he retorted. 'So don't waste it arguing with me. An evil witch has struck out at Oscar and Benji. I am *not* leaving your side, not even for a moment.'

I huffed but recognised the futility of arguing.

'I'll go door to door,' Oscar said. 'And I'll recruit others to help.' He pulled on his pyjama top and padded barefoot into the corridor. He left the door open so we could hear as he pounded on Ethan's door.

Ethan opened it. 'Oscar?' He took in his appearance. 'What's wrong?'

'I was poisoned last night. Are Jacob and Henry okay?'

Ethan's lips thinned. 'Jacob is. Henry didn't come home last night.' He turned back into the apartment. 'Jacob! We need to find Henry! NOW!'

The three men started knocking on doors and I left them to it. I took the stairs to my apartment, Bastion one step behind me. It was time to see if a highly illegal grimoire had another miracle for me.

And if he did, I didn't care what rules it broke to use it.

Chapter 15

I didn't even try to persuade Bastion to let me out of his sight; I just went straight in my bedroom to my safe. 'Close the curtains,' I instructed briskly as I unlocked it and pulled out the grimoire.

I stroked a finger down Grimmy's spine but nothing happened. I pulled my athame from its ankle holster, pricked my finger and let the blood well up. When a good drop had gathered, I stroked my finger again down the stained spine. Bastion said nothing.

The book rose up, shining with a golden light. 'Why hello, Miss Amber. And what can I—' He paused mid-sentence. 'You have the griffin with you.' To my surprise there was absolutely none of Grimmy's usual Anti-Crea vitriol in his voice.

'I do. We have an emergency. Do you know of another way to reactivate a golem? He's already been out for

Goddess knows how long, and we're too far away from Edinburgh's activation chambers.'

Grimmy's pages fluttered in agitation as he scrolled through them to see if there was anything that could help Benji. I held my breath. When his pages stuttered and stopped, my heart sank. 'There is nothing here,' he said finally.

I sat on the floor in despair, tears welling in my eyes. Bastion dropped down next to me and wrapped his arms around me. What was the point in magic if I couldn't save Benji? A sob escaped.

'Don't despair, Miss Amber,' Grimmy said. 'There is nothing in my pages that will help us, but I do have an idea. There are two golems in existence at present, yes?'

I palmed the tears from my cheeks and clung to his words. If I had hope – any hope – then it was better than nothing. I'd do anything to see Benji breathing again. 'Yes,' I confirmed, pulling myself together. 'David and Benji.'

'Then, Miss Amber, you must bring me David as fast as you can,' Grimmy ordered.

I felt sick as I realised what his solution must be. 'You can't hurt David to save Benji. Benji would never forgive himself.' Saving Benji at David's expense – Benji would rather die than that. But by the Goddess, it was tempting.

Had I not just thought that I would do *anything* to see Benji alive again?

Grimmy harrumphed. 'Oh ye of little faith, Miss Amber. I am burned by the insinuation that I would harm the other golem. He will not be harmed, but you need to bring him here. And Miss Amber?'

'Yes?'

'Do it quickly.' Grimmy shut his pages and fell back on the bed. I hastily shoved the grimoire back into the safe and closed it with a clank.

Bastion could fly to Edinburgh and back to get David, or we could just get David to travel to us as fast as he could, or we could lug Benji to Edinburgh... But all of those options would cost us precious hours that we couldn't afford. Every moment of deactivation meant it was less likely we'd bring back Benji. We might awaken him, but he wouldn't be the golem we'd known.

I pulled out my phone and rang Kass.

'Good morning, Amber, how are you?' Her voice was strained and I could tell that today was not a good pain day for her. I really needed to finish her fibromyalgia potion, dammit, but it would have to wait until I didn't have emergencies pouring out of my ears.

'I need to borrow David right now. Tell him to go to the surface and stand by the sign for The Witchery. A vampyr will bring him to me. It's an emergency. Can you do that?'

'Of course—'

As I hung up I hoped she'd forgive me my rudeness, but I had no time to waste on idle chatter. I rang the next number and prayed the asshole would pick up. I'd spent my life making powerful allies; here's hoping this one came through.

'Voltaire,' he answered, as if I didn't know who I'd dialled.

'I'm closing in on the evil Coven, but I need a favour, *now*. Go to Edinburgh, to the Witchery. Grab the golem standing by the sign and bring him to the shadows outside my Coven tower.'

There was a pause while he thought about it. 'You'll cut me in when you have found another evil witch?'

'I will,' I promised, hating myself for dealing with the devil. 'Bring me the golem.'

I hung up and touched the walls of my apartment, stretching my awareness outwards until I could feel the walls of the whole tower. I waited for the telltale feeling of a golem, the feeling of earth and magic on an autumn morning.

I kept my awareness half in the wards even as I rang down to the concierge's desk. 'A golem is approaching. Let him in and show him up to Oscar's apartment. Now!'

I hung up, grabbed Grimmy from the safe and made tracks downstairs with Bastion close on my heels. As I started down, Bastion shifted into griffin form. 'Get on,' he said.

I clung onto his fur and tried not to shriek as he leapt onto the railings then plummeted down to the second floor. It was far faster than running down the flights of stairs, but it sure sent my heart pounding. When we reached our destination, he landed lightly and I climbed off.

Bastion shifted back to human form and we ran to Oscar's apartment where Benji was still standing – frozen, cold and alone.

Chapter 16

'We're coming,' I said to my friend as I touched his cold flesh. 'Just hang on a moment longer.' I pushed down panic and anxiety, because it had no place here. I was here to *save* Benji and I wouldn't entertain any other outcome.

I hefted up Grimmy and stroked his spine. He instantly rose up, like he'd been waiting impatiently. When he sensed the golem, his pages flipped erratically. 'Why, no you don't, you big lug,' he murmured to Benji. 'We're going to fix you right up, young sir – with one little change.'

'What change?' I demanded. 'How can you save him?'

'The activation crystal buried within him is fractured and the magic is leaking out. We need a new source of life for our friend.'

Despair washed through me. 'And how will we do that?' Then a chill took me. Grimmy had promised no harm would come to David, but how else could he be planning to save Benji apart from ripping David's crystal from him?

'I happen to know a great source of life,' Grimmy said.

'You're not taking David's crystal!'

He huffed. 'Miss Amber, you and I are going to have a lengthy conversation about how little regard you have for me, but later. After our young Benjamin has been saved.'

There was a knock and Ethan and Oscar came in with David following behind them. At the sight of Benji, he let out a rumbling roar of rage. 'Benji!'

'We're going to save him!' I said. 'But we need your help.'

'Just name it,' David snarled. 'He is my friend.'

'He is,' I agreed. I flicked my eyes to Ethan who was still hovering by the door. His gaze was fixed on the living book hovering in the air. Crud. 'You found Henry?' I asked to distract him.

He met my eyes and looked rueful. 'Yes, with Sarah.'

I winced. 'Ouch.'

'Yes. I'll be discussing the importance of fidelity with him later. I will leave you to ... whatever this is.' He gave me a nod, then stepped out and shut the door behind him. Bother: I could have done without him seeing the illegal grimoire. Sometimes Ethan was a bit of a stickler for the rules, but now wasn't the time to worry about it. I'd deal with any repercussions later.

I turned to Grimmy. 'What is this? What are we going to do?'

'You don't know?' David asked in surprise.

'As nuts as it is, the book is calling the shots,' I said wryly, aware I sounded a bit crazy. 'Now, Grimmy, come clean. How are we saving our Benji?'

'I should think that would have been obvious to someone with your fine brain, Miss Amber. We'll use me.'

My mine went blank. 'What?'

'We'll use *me*,' he repeated. 'You may recall some time ago that you thrust me into your friend here for safe keeping after an ill-advised jaunt to Edinburgh. Benjamin held me safe, and whilst I was within his body I found I could see and hear everything around me. Not sense it, Miss Amber, but *see* it with Benjamin's own eyes. I do declare, for the first time, I could *see*.

' It was an experience that altered me and my perception of the world around me profoundly. When you had to shut Benjamin down, I protected the crystal within him so that it did not shatter as it normally would do in a deactivation. Consequently, you were able to reactivate him.

'This time, I was not there to save him, but I sense an opportunity both for me and for him. If I join with him, we can use *my* magic to power him. As you know, I have bartered with your ancestors, giving them spells and potions and runes in exchange for their very life force. I have within me at least a century of life force. I propose to share it with Benjamin.'

Grimmy twisted in the air to face towards David. 'Young man, you must thrust me within your friend and align me with his heart crystal. I will do the rest.'

David blinked once, then grabbed the floating book. Before I could even think of an objection, he thrust my sentient grimoire clean into Benji's chest.

Chapter 17

There was a silence that dragged slowly on. As nothing happened, I wondered whether we needed the power of the runes and the awakening potions to bring Benji back to life. Maybe Grimmy's life force alone wasn't enough to kick-start the golem.

Unfortunately, it takes weeks to brew the awakening potions. Luckily there was a potion mistress in Edinburgh whose sole job it was to keep those two volatile potions ready in case the Council needed a golem in a hurry. There was always a golem ready at any one time to be woken up, and I had no doubt that some acolytes were beavering away under someone's watchful gaze building another body now that we'd awakened both Benji *and* David. I could travel to Edinburgh to get the potions, but I feared that any further delay would be too much for Benji *and* Grimmy.

The aching silence continued and I reached out to grasp Bastion's hand. His solid presence comforted me, even as despair crept in. I clenched my teeth. No! It wasn't fair. I had lost too much and I would *not* lose Benji. I couldn't. He was such a golden soul that he deserved to live more than many others that walked this Earth.

As always in moments of despair, I turned to my Goddess. Inspiration struck and I grasped the pendant around my neck. Why hadn't I thought of using it before? Stupid!

'*Sisters,*' I entreated silently. '*What can be done?*'

'*Touch the pendant to the golem, Princess. If the Goddess wills it, she will assist in this matter. There will be a cost,*' Abigay's voice said. Despite the warning her words gave me a flash of hope.

'*I'll pay it gladly if it will bring Benji back,*' I replied desperately. I let go of Bastion's hand and stepped closer to Benji, lifted the necklace from my neck and placed the pendant flush against his chest.

There was a flash of bright white light and Benji groaned. Relief flooded me as his eyes opened. For a moment, they shone with the white light of the Goddess but then it faded.

Benji blinked and looked at me, and his wide innocent smile beamed across his face. 'You saved me, Am Bam!'

Then he grimaced. 'Why now, Mr Benjamin, we cannot be calling a refined witch – the Crone no less – "Am Bam". That is just not dignified.' I blinked as the refined southern accent fell from Benji's lips. Well, I guess that answered the question as to whether or not Grimmy had survived the amalgamation into Benji.

'Grimmy!' I gasped, more relieved than I expected that the book was still with us – albeit trapped inside Benji.

'Quite,' he said, his tone also relieved. 'It seems I have survived the transition from book to golem.'

'Benji?' I asked urgently. 'Are you still okay in there?'

His expression was open and delighted. 'I am! I'm fine, Am Bam. Mr Grimmy saved my life. I am very grateful to him.'

'As am I,' I admitted.

David was gaping. 'So now there's two of you in there?'

'I've always liked the idea of a roommate,' Benji said shyly. 'I have very much enjoyed living with Oscar.'

Oscar stepped forward and clapped the golem into a hug. 'As I have with you, Benji. I am so relieved to see you're okay.'

Benji hugged Oscar back and that made my eyes well up. I hadn't seen Oscar hug anyone ever besides me or Mum.

Bastion's arms wrapped around me and I let the scent of him settle me. We'd been through hell and back, and it wasn't even 9am. I dreaded to think what the rest of the day would bring.

Chapter 18

'It has occurred to me that Grimmy is not a very dignified name,' Grimmy complained. 'Now that I have a proper body, I believe that I should have a proper name.'

'What do you propose?' I asked the grimoire with interest. Of all the names in the world to choose from, what would he pick? My money was on something posh and pretentious – Archibald maybe, or Percival.

He thought for a moment. 'I expect we will want to keep my residence within Benji's body somewhat secret. Discretion is advised. As such, I propose that I am referred to as Benjamin, whilst my compatriot here is named Benji, thus differentiating between us without ever drawing attention to our new situation.'

I blinked. That was actually a very good idea.

'Brilliant idea!' Benji enthused. 'Do you like rock music?'

'I must confess, I have no idea,' the newly named Benjamin responded. 'I have been exposed to very little of the arts, musical or otherwise.'

'We'll change that,' Benji promised. 'There are some beautiful things to see in this world. I'll share them with you.'

There was a pause, and when Benjamin spoke his voice was thick with emotion. 'I would truly appreciate that, my young friend.'

And now I felt like a witch with a B for being so mean to ... Benjamin. I cleared my throat. 'I'm sorry to interrupt the moment, I really am, but there are some important things we need to discuss. The most pressing of which is, do you know who attacked you?'

Benji grimaced. 'I'm sorry, I don't know what happened. I was drinking with our Coven—' the 'our' made me smile— 'and then in the night I heard Oscar cry out. Sometimes his nightmares bother him and I went to offer comfort, as friends should. As I stood up, I felt funny. Suddenly I couldn't move and then everything just – stopped.' He shrugged. 'I don't know what happened. I've never heard of a golem being poisoned before.'

'Just because it hasn't happened before doesn't mean it isn't possible,' I murmured, my brain whirring.

I glanced at my watch; it was just gone 9am. I'd lost my chance to confront Hannah in the privacy of her own rooms, but it couldn't be helped. We had Benji back, and that was everything. 'We need to go the potions lab and confront Hannah,' I said.

'Why Hannah?' Benji asked curiously.

'She is the only other witch I have told about the circus where Meredith and Ria were attacked. She *has* to be the one who painted the cancelling runes there. It stands to reason that she is also to blame for the attacks on you and Oscar.' I couldn't cope if I had even *more* evil witches amongst us.

'Or she told someone else about it,' Bastion said, playing devil's advocate.

'No,' I disagreed. 'Hannah swore an oath. If she told anyone about it, the geas would kick in and kill her. She knew the severity of the oath that I had extracted from her and she wouldn't risk an oath death. She wouldn't gossip about it over a glass of wine.'

'You could have been followed to the circus one time,' Benji suggested.

Oscar shook his head. 'I have been trained to spot a tail. We've had them a number of times but I've always lost them before we reached our destination. It's possible, I suppose, but not probable.'

'Well, let's see what she says,' Benji said. He looked unhappy. 'I've always liked Hannah.'

'Me too.' I sighed softly. 'Me too.'

We climbed the stairs to the third floor. The potions lab was dark and when I flicked on the lights no one was there; a few cauldrons were covered and runed into stasis, but other than that, the place was empty.

Hannah's workstation was completely clear. I frowned. Hannah was organised; she always came down the night before to prep her ingredients and her workstation to maximise her brewing time the next day. She was a creature of habit and eager to please; I hated the thought that perhaps she had been eager to please the wrong person. If she hadn't prepped her workspace, maybe it was because she knew the jig was up. After all, it wouldn't take a genius to realise I'd be taking a hard look at her after the circus was attacked, and she'd had no alibi through work, though I supposed she might offer another excuse for her absence.

'Let's go to her room,' I said tightly. '2C.' We turned off the lights, trooped back down the stairs and knocked on her door. There was no response.

'Hannah?' I called through the door. 'It's Amber. I need to speak to you.' Still no response.

'I'll remove the wards.' Bastion's eyes glowed as he carefully removed the wards from her door. 'There are two magical signatures,' he warned, 'and one of the wards was a containment one.'

As he ripped them away it became clear what the containment rune was for. A terrible odour started to fill the corridor. Bastion looked at me, his eyes sympathetic.

I knew that smell, too. It was the stench of death.

Chapter 19

Bastion turned politely to Benji. 'Would you like to kick the door down? You need to put your boot just here.' He pointed to a part of the door beside the lock.

Benji nodded, his expression serious. 'I would like that.' He reared back and kicked. The door flew off its hinges and landed with a thump onto the sofa inside the room.

'Maybe a little less force next time,' Bastion said lightly, but he grinned and clapped Benji on the shoulder. 'Good job.' Benji beamed at the praise.

'I want to kick in a door,' David complained.

'Next time,' I promised vaguely, busy thinking about what I would find inside the apartment. For some reason, my feet didn't want to move forward. Death awaited me in there; the only question was who had died? I didn't want to find out.

Bastion moved forward to check the room was safe before I entered, and that was enough to galvanise me into action. When he called the all-clear, his voice grim, I strode in. I would not be cowed.

He was in the bedroom, so I followed him there. The stench thickened and I had to work hard not to cover my nose and mouth with my sleeve. Instead I breathed shallowly through my mouth.

Hannah lay on her bed, tied down and spread-eagled. She had been wearing nightclothes but the shirt had been wrenched open and she had been cruelly sliced into. Her whole body was dusted black, covered with the shadows of an oath death. In the end, she had broken her oath under torture.

An oath death had taken her, but looking at the cruel marks on her body I knew it was not her fault. Anyone would have broken with the agony she must have suffered. She hadn't betrayed me, not knowingly, not willingly. I struggled to hold it together.

I tried to examine the body critically, battling to shove my emotions into a box somewhere deep inside me. This was *Hannah.* I had been so proud of her and I had identified with her so strongly. She was so hardworking, and her future was so damned bright. Or it had been.

Damn it, I would not cry here. She deserved to have me witness her suffering and I would not balk at it.

'Can you cut her free?' I asked Bastion tightly. I hated seeing her bound and prostrate like that.

His hands shifted to claws and he effortlessly cut the ties that held her down. There was no point worrying about preserving the scene because I wouldn't be reporting this to the Connection. It was an in-house matter – and when I found out who had done this to her, I was going to plunge my athame into their cursed heart.

I swallowed hard, stepped forward and picked up Hannah's hand. The muscles flexed and moved; rigor mortis had come and gone, which meant she had died between one and four days ago. The blood on the sheets had dried, so she'd probably been dead at least a couple of days. The containment spell had kept the scent of blood, death and faeces locked in the room.

The horrific signs of torture on her body told me that she hadn't willingly given up the circus, and tears filled my eyes despite my best intentions. I had been thinking the worst about her and all this time she'd been lying dead all those floors below.

'Edward,' I said suddenly as my brain clicked into gear. I blinked away the useless wetness in my eyes. 'Edward gave you and Benji drinks. He was supposed to guard her so there's no way that he didn't contact her for two days.' He hadn't been on my suspect list because he was a wizard rather than a witch, but that didn't mean he couldn't work for the evil witches.

'I'm on it,' Oscar growled.

'I'm coming with you,' Benji said fiercely. 'This is not right.'

'It is wrong,' David agreed. 'I will also help capture this Edward.'

'We need to question him,' I said firmly. 'Bring him to me alive.'

The three men nodded and left me alone with Bastion and Hannah. She was in her late twenties but in death she looked painfully young. I looked around but there was no sign of Fifi, her blue corn snake familiar. 'I'm sorry Hannah,' I murmured aloud. 'I failed you.'

'You did not,' Bastion snarled. 'How many times must I tell you that you are not responsible for the actions of those around you? All you can do is control your own behaviour. You did nothing wrong.'

'I believed the worst of her,' I said in a small voice. 'I thought that she had betrayed us.'

'Because the evidence suggested she had,' he argued. 'You are only human, Amber. You can only follow the evidence.'

Intellectually I knew he was right, but emotionally I was battered. 'Can you cover her?' I asked as my voice broke. 'I can't look at her anymore.' I would, though; I would see her every time I closed my eyes for many months to come.

Bastion picked up the duvet, which was strewn across the floor, and laid it over her. At first glance she could have been asleep, but she wasn't. She was dead and she would never fulfil the potential that had bubbled out of her.

Then I let go. I fell to my knees and wept.

Chapter 20

With Jeb dead, we didn't have anyone in the maintenance role. We needed to recruit someone, I thought dully. For now, I called Ethan and Jacob.

Bastion carefully carried Hannah down the steps to the cremator and laid her body on the metal table next to it. When Jeb had died, we had unceremoniously burned his body as quickly as possible in case the evil Coven decided to reanimate his corpse for one last 'eff you'. Hannah deserved ceremony: last rites and a funeral.

I would send a Coven-wide email later but for now it was time to come clean about a few horrific facts. There were too many secrets, too many lies. How could I govern a Coven whilst I lied to it? How could I hunt the evil within when I trusted no one?

Now that Hannah's body was taken care of, stored safely, we locked the huge incineration room and headed back to her flat. Ethan had arrived and was standing in Jacob's arms; both had obviously been crying. 'What happened?' he demanded, stepping back, shoulders squared. 'Hannah?'

'Hannah knew some important information,' I explained evenly. 'She was tortured to reveal it. When she broke, an oath death took her.'

'We will not let the records hold her an oath breaker,' Jacob said fiercely.

'No,' I agreed. 'We will not.' I waited a beat. 'Now that Jeb is dead, we need someone else to deal with this—' I cut myself off before I could say 'mess'. Hannah wasn't a mess. 'Deal with this,' I said instead.

'I will see to it,' Jacob promised.

'Jay... ' Ethan started.

'Hush. It is my choice. I will clean up Hannah's room – she deserves that. I will pack up her belongings. She has a sister, Jennifer, in Liverpool who will want to look through them.'

Jennifer: I hadn't even thought of Hannah's sister. When Hannah had joined us, I'd offered a place to her sister too, but she hadn't taken it. Hannah had been quietly relieved, ready to strike out on her own. But now I would have to tell Jennifer about her sister's death. Sometimes being a leader was the worst.

I nodded my approval of Jacob's kind offer. 'Thank you, Jacob. I have looked, but there is no sign of Fifi.'

Jacob swore aloud. 'To take her familiar...' He shook his head as tears welled again. 'These bastards are monsters. She will have to be burned alone.'

'I know.' I sighed. 'I will do everything I can to find Fifi, then we will scatter her ashes with Hannah's in our garden. They *will* be together.'

Jacob set his jaw into a grim line. 'Yes, so mote it be.'

'So mote it be,' I responded fiercely. 'Ethan, we need a meeting in the Coven common room. Everyone is to attend, regardless of their work commitments. We will tell them about Hannah's death then go immediately to the incinerator room to say goodbye. Can you arrange food and drinks for a wake afterwards? And the Farewell Elixir?'

Ethan nodded briskly. 'What time?'

'Four pm for the meet,' I suggested.

'Consider it done.'

I touched his arm lightly. 'I do.' I gave him a squeeze and then walked away. That was probably the closest I'd managed to come to saying I trusted him. He and I had never gelled, but that didn't mean I didn't have faith in him to do what was right. Then again, I had trusted Jeb and been completely wrong about that. Maybe my judgement wasn't all that it was cracked up to be.

Bastion and I excused ourselves and went up to my flat. Oscar, Benji and David were sitting inside and I raised an eyebrow in question – they were supposed to be finding Edward.

Oscar grimaced and shook his head. 'He's gone. His apartment was cleaned out.'

'Super clean,' David added. 'It smelled funny.'

'Bleach,' Oscar explained. 'He didn't want to leave a stray hair or drop of blood to be used against him. I checked the security footage in the car park. He left at 3am, a bag over his shoulder.'

I scrubbed at my eyes. 'So there's no doubt that he wasn't coerced.'

'He certainly strolled out alone,' Benji confirmed.

'With a certain amount of swagger, too, I should say,' Benjamin drawled.

Bastion pushed me gently into a seat and went to put the kettle on. He moved soundlessly around the kitchen; the deadliest assassin in the world was bustling around my kitchen making tea. Sometimes life was weird.

We sat in silence, each lost in our own thoughts. I sipped my hot brew out of a cup that said *If it was legal to marry food, I'd still choose you over pizza*. It made me smile. It was definitely a Bastion mug because mine were all decidedly bitchier. For himself, Bastion had picked one that said *Some drink from the fountain of knowledge; you only gargled.*

I let my eyes gaze into the middle distance. I was looking towards a painting above the TV, one of Mum's more chaotic pictures, a black-and-white image of a dark staircase spiralling downwards. Numbers and letters interspersed the steps.

Her words suddenly echoed in my head: '*It's in the painting*'. Not in *this* painting, but *the* painting. She hadn't been talking about the painting in her hallway but this one. I was sure of it.

I set my mug down and pushed myself up. Holy heck. Grabbing a pen and paper, I stood in front of the picture and wrote down the sequence of numbers and letters as they went down the staircase, then I ran into my office and booted up my computer. Bastion followed me silently.

I double-clicked on the CD. When the box popped up asking for a password, I put in the series of letters and numbers. Rather than the instant denial we'd been having, the 'working' icon appeared. My heart was racing.

Abruptly the icon disappeared and in its place was a folder full of documents.

My hands shook and I clicked to open the first file. It was entitled *For Amber*.

Chapter 21

Mum's image filled the screen. She looked young and vibrant, her hair a lustrous red with not a hint of grey. I was looking at the mum of my childhood some thirty years ago.

She scrambled back from the video camera and sat on a chair. 'Hi, Amber,' she said and her eyes softened. 'I'm sorry to leave you this video. I hope it's not necessary, but if you're watching this...' She took a deep breath. 'I don't know where to start,' she muttered to herself. She looked into the camera again. 'It's so hard to squint into the future and see you, Am. You're so young and conscientious, so hardworking. I'm putting a lot on your shoulders and I am desperately sorry for it.'

She blew out a breath. 'There was a prophecy. As you know, prophecies are normally read at birth but when we took you to the seers when you were a babe, they said that there were too many paths in front of you. You needed to come back when you were older, when some choices had already been made.

'I was planning to take you again when you hit puberty, but instead we bumped into Melva at the Spice Shoppe and she recited a prophecy there and then. I'll recite it as best as I can recall.'

She closed her eyes and intoned:

'Through the veils of time, a mother's plight
Her mind is the cost to set things right.
She weaves the threads of fate so tight
Her sacrifice made in love's pure light.
A griffin's wings on the loyal guide,
A familiar bond, forever tied.
Protecting as the fates decide
In shadows cast as realms collide.
The Witch, the Crone, her destiny clear,
Black witches tremble when she's near.
With heart and rune, she'll persevere,
In a hunt for justice, she'll have no peer.
But lurking deep within the night,
The Coven's head, her father's might.
A reckoning waits in close sight,
A clash of dark and radiant light

So heed the hidden prophecy spun

Of time, protectors and battles won.

The Crone shall rise like the sun

To face her father, darkness undone.'

Mum cleared her throat. 'Okay, so what does it all mean? Well, first it meant I had to take a hard look at your father. All those evenings he'd been away for work suddenly took on a sinister tone. I hired a PI who took photos of him doing terrible things, horrific things. Don't look at the photos, Amber. Get someone else to look for you, if you have someone you trust.'

She bit her lip. 'I really hope you have someone to trust. If you don't, you have my word that you can trust the griffin known as Bastion. I swear he has your best interests at heart.' She paused, clearly warring with herself.

'He's your familiar, Amber,' she blurted out. 'I'm sorry, I'm *so* sorry. Maybe I did wrong keeping it from you ... but a creature as a familiar? It hasn't happened in centuries, and every single witch in history that's had a creature familiar has turned into a black witch. I'm sure that won't happen with you, but I've taken steps to make sure that the bond with Bastion won't be known to you during your formative years. You already have so much to overcome. You don't need this too.'

She took a deep breath. Lucille frolicked around her feet, kicking up her little legs as she ran around mum's chair. Mum watched with a soft smile on her face. It faded as she sighed again.

'You deserve joy like this,' she said, gesturing unhappily to Lucille. 'I don't know if I've made the right decision, but I swear I'm trying to do everything right by you. When I found out what your father had done, I had to take steps to protect us from him. I needed something to ensure he wouldn't ever harm us.'

She paused dramatically. 'Amber, I found out that his black Coven had made a harkan.' A harkan was an object of power. It was made by collecting one drop of blood at a time from a murder victim then crystallising the drops through magic. The bigger the crystal, the more deaths were required to make it and the greater the power it held. Rumour had it that the owner of a harkan crystal never needed recharge in the Common realm.

Her voice filled with horror. 'It was so big, Amber.' She shook her head. 'I hired a wizard to help me get in and out of the Coven and steal the crystal.' Her wry smile suggested it had been far from easy. 'But we did it. And then what? I had the harkan, and I knew the black Coven would come for me – come for the crystal.'

She sighed. 'I consulted with Grimmy. He told me the only way to protect the crystal was to bind it to me and my bloodline. If they tried to take it, it wouldn't work for them the way they wanted or needed. And if they tried to use it there would be dire consequences for them.' She said that with grim satisfaction.

'I made sure that Shaun knew only you or I could use it properly. He will have to keep us both safe – or you, at least. He's not the leader of the black Coven at the moment, but the prophecy said he will be. He'll work his way up the ranks so he can protect us and, by extension, the harkan.

'Don't get emotional about his motivation, Am. He wants power.' Her voice was bitter. 'You can't do what he's done if you don't crave power. So I stole the harkan, and with Grimmy's help I bound it to me. And to you. To do that, I gave it sentience.' She hesitated. 'To bind it, I had to add to it.'

I stared at the screen, aghast. To add to the harkan, my mum *had* to have killed someone. I felt sick. Not only had my mum added to the harkan, Grimmy had *known* all this time?

She licked her lips. 'I've hidden it. To bind it to me, I had to give it part of my mind and my soul. I can already feel that I am – less. I suddenly find I need to make notes all the time, and my memory can't be trusted. With time – and if the harkan is used – the effects will worsen. I don't know how long we have.'

She shook her head. 'I'm sorry, I truly am. I had your mind cleared. I couldn't risk that you might have seen your father do something dark, that he'd already started grooming you to become a black witch.' Her voice softened. 'And I wanted to ease your hurt, baby girl. You were crying for him so much and it killed me because he *chose* this. He *chose* to hurt and kill people for power.'

'Don't waste your tears on him, Amber. All the time he had us, he had another family – another wife, other kids, Rebecca and Edward. Half-siblings I have no intention of ever letting you meet. They had a third child, but he died. Shaun's other wife is a black witch, too. She has embraced the darkness just like he has. I sometimes wonder if the child died of illness – or something far worse.'

She grimaced and tightened her lips. 'I rue the day I ever met Shaun Bolton. I will protect you from him until my dying breath, Amber. And now, he will do the same,' she said with grim satisfaction, 'because only you or I can fully wield the power of their Goddess-forsaken harkan. And the black Coven knows it.'

Chapter 22

I suddenly remembered Becky – Rebecca – telling me that her father had ordered the Coven not to harm me, and that he'd been furious when she'd tried to bomb me. At the time I had thought he must still feel some sort of paternal affection for me, but in truth it had all been about the harkan crystal.

My father was protecting his investment, not me. Placing Jeb in my Coven to woo me, to win me over to the dark side, was just another ploy to get me to help him. I felt sick.

'Hey,' Bastion murmured. 'Come here.' He lifted me out of the chair, sat down with me on his lap and wrapped his arms around me. He didn't utter any empty platitudes about how everything would be all right; he just let me fall apart, his solid presence promising he'd be here to help me pick up the pieces.

I let Bastion look at the pictures and he agreed with Mum's assessment that I shouldn't see them. They were an extra source of blackmail, nothing more.

There was also a data file with Shaun's date of birth, National Insurance number and all his previous addresses. Mum had compiled a full family tree, outlining three generations of relatives. She'd noted who his friends were, though there was a small NB from mum that she couldn't assume any of them were evil witches.

Bastion showed me one photo, a picture of Shaun and his other wife with Becky and Edward as kids. I didn't recognise the wife but I did recognise Edward. The name and his cursed actions should have been a clue, but for some reason I hadn't realised that Edward was my half-brother until that moment.

I frowned. 'But he's a wizard.'

'So is Louisa.' At my blank expression Bastion clarified, 'The wife.'

Crikey, Shaun sure liked to surround himself with Ls: Louisa, Luna and Lucille.

My eyebrows rose. 'So much for magical purity, then.' The evil Coven was one of those organisations that propounded the virtues of magical purity, or so the bedtime stories said.

Bastion shrugged. 'We all make different choices when we're in love.'

I wanted to ask Bastion if he had ever been in love; it seemed unlikely that he hadn't during two centuries of living. I'd had him and Jake – and I was only in my forties. I didn't ask, though; I wasn't brave enough and this wasn't the right moment.

'Hard to imagine my father and "love" in the same sentence,' I said instead.

'He loves *you*,' Bastion disagreed. 'He wanted you safe at the auction house.'

I snorted. 'Because of the harkan! He wants me to unlock its full potential, and I couldn't do that from a Connection jail cell – or if they'd killed me by mistake.'

'Maybe,' he conceded. 'But things are rarely black or white.'

'Bastion, I do believe you are an optimist.'

He clapped a hand to his heart. 'You wound me!' he joked, making me smile. His smile faded. 'What do you want to do now, Bambi?'

I huffed a breath. 'I want to go and shout at Oscar, and kick the ass of that duplicitous grimoire, but as he is currently residing in my dear friend Benji I'll give him a firm telling off instead. And Oscar can have a ticking off, too.'

'Oscar has already been through a lot,' Bastion pointed out gently.

'Maybe so, but the damned grimoire hasn't.'

I jumped off Bastion's lap and marched out of my office to confront my grimoire, who had helped persuade my mum that giving a piece of her mind and soul to a cursed crystal was a *good* idea.

Chapter 23

I strode into the living room, full of righteous fury. 'Am Bam? Are you okay?' Benji asked apprehensively as I stood in front of him, glowering with my hands on my hips.

'I am very angry, but not at you. I am angry with Benjamin. Come out, you bastard, and talk to me.'

'Why Miss Amber, I declare that is not the nicest way to address me,' Benjamin said. 'Though technically, as I have no mother or father, I suppose they cannot have borne me in wedlock and thus the description may be technically correct.'

'You told my mum to give a piece of herself to the bloody harkan crystal!'

'Ah,' he said urbanely. 'That. Yes, well. It was the only solution to her particular problem.'

'She *added* to the harkan,' I spat in horror. Her confession made me sick to my stomach; she had killed someone and used their life force to add to the damned crystal.

'She did, but not in the way in which you are imagining,' Benjamin said. 'She found a terminally ill patient called Diane on a crossover ward and explained what she needed to do and why. The elderly lady agreed to help her. She checked herself out of hospital and came to our Coven. She wanted her death to *matter*. And truly, it did.'

'No matter which way you dress it up, Mum killed someone. And she used their death in her magic.' I felt sick.

'Yes, she did,' Oscar said softly. 'And it ate her up inside to the point that she went back in time to try and undo it. She used the portal to go back to persuade Diane not to go with her. She went back to a time a few hours before she'd met with her, explained what would happen, begged Diane not to do it. Diane smiled and nodded, and when the then-present Luna came and told her of her plan, Diane *still* went with her anyway.'

The wind went out of my sails. '*That* was why she used the Third realm?'

Oscar nodded. 'She went back to try and stop what she'd already put in motion. But you can't change what has already happened.'

'The fixity of time,' I muttered.

'Indeed.'

Mum had made some poor decisions. Wiping my memory, killing Diane and adding to the crystal... I should have been furious with her but, truthfully, she had already been punished enough. Giving a piece of herself to the crystal was foolhardy – surely she could have found another way? But it was done and could not be undone. Mum's jaunt through time was evidence of that.

I had thought that the first verse of the prophecy was so clear, but those thrice-damned seers – with them nothing was ever quite how you thought it was.

Through the veils of time, a mother's plight; Her mind is the cost to set things right. She weaves the threads of fate so tight. Her sacrifice made in love's pure light. I had thought the reference to time had meant Mum's use of the Third realm, that her mind had been the price for using that, but the two sentences were unconnected.

Mum's plight had been a moral one; her distress over killing Diane had sent her back through time. Her mind was the cost of securing the harkan, keeping it from being fully used by the evil Coven. Her sacrifice – giving a piece of her mind and soul – had been made because she loved me. She had been trying to keep me safe from my father and the evil Coven.

I sat down. How could I be angry? Mum had lost everything for me. I could even forgive her the ill-advised clearing – she was my mum and I could forgive her anything. Frankly, if she told me now that she'd killed someone, I would help her hide the body. Love makes you do crazy things, including breaking your own rules. There was nothing I wouldn't do for love and I couldn't fault my mum for feeling the same, even with all the grief it had brought down on our heads.

Coulda, woulda, shoulda had no place in my life. All I could do now was move forward. And that is exactly what I was going to do.

Chapter 24

The Coven common room was full but eerily silent. A Coven-wide summons like this was rare, especially during the working day. All eyes were on me and the tension was palpable. Everyone gathered there knew that what I was about to say would not be good news. You could have heard the rune stones drop such was the strength of the silence.

I touched the pentagram pendant that hung at my neck and felt a surge of affection and confidence through it. My sisters believed in me. I felt confidence from inside too, from myself and from Bastion. He believed in me, too.

I cleared my throat and broke the silence. Best deliver the news like ripping off a plaster, I decided. 'Brace yourselves. It's time for some hard truths. Firstly, Hannah Lions is dead.'

Gasps and wails rose from the assembled witches. They paired up to offer comfort, pulling the nearest person into hugs of misery and commiseration. Hannah had been popular with good reason; she had been kind, friendly and hardworking.

I let my Coven have a moment of disbelief and mourning but my news bulletin was not done, far from it. The hits had to keep on coming. I waited until there was a lull in the noise, and spoke again. 'Secondly, the black Coven, the evil Coven, is real.' Shocked silence fell. 'They killed the former Crone, Abigay. I have been tasked with rooting them out.'

I took the time to look around and meet the eyes of those assembled there. 'Thirdly, Ria and Meredith were targeted by them, and that was why Cindy was killed.'

'I *KNEW* it!' Melrose snarled. 'I *knew* Ria and Meredith wouldn't miss Cindy's funeral. Where are they?'

'With Hannah's help, I hid them in a safe house,' I replied calmly, mixing a little lie with the truth. I wouldn't risk the circus, even for my Coven. 'Hannah was tortured and killed to ascertain their location.'

'Good Goddess above,' Melrose gasped. 'Are they—'

'Meredith was attacked but we managed to save her. Ria is fine. They have been moved to another location.'

'Who?' Melrose gasped. 'Who would kill Hannah? She was the best of us.' She sobbed the last few words.

'She was,' I agreed. 'All evidence points to Edward Tenby being the one who killed her.'

Murmurs of 'her own guard' circulated around the common room as they digested the horrific news. In for a penny, in for a pound. 'Jeb's death was not accidental. He was a necromancer working for the evil Coven. He was responsible for High Priestess Melva's death.'

More gasps and wails. I tried to stifle my impatience; this was a lot of dreadful, upsetting news, a news bulletin full of deaths and betrayals. I looked for anyone who *didn't* look genuinely upset, anyone who *didn't* look shocked.

There was no surprise on either Ethan's or Jacob's faces, but they knew all about it already. Henry and Sarah were cosied up together close to his fathers. Henry looked a little smug, though that might have been due to the nubile young woman pressed against him rather than any dark inclinations on his part.

John had his arm around Venice; his eyes were grim but he didn't look particularly shocked. Timothy was next to Briony and he didn't look particularly emotional, either. Toxic masculinity at work? Or something more? Goddess,

I hated this. Looking at everyone as though evil might be in their hearts and their actions was draining.

Enough time had passed and I needed to move this along. 'As you know, Hilary Mitchell was an evil witch. I fear that the evil Coven's rot has spread insidiously. Guard your hearts and minds. Do not give into temptation to use pain to boost your powers – greater power is not worth your soul. Examine your companions and watch their actions. Any suspicions, please consult me. As you know, it is my job as the Crone to root out evil wherever it exists – here or in the council.'

I paused then went on. 'As such, this is my notice to you that I will be stepping down as Coven Mother. I will serve a week or two's notice and will shortly be opening the application and interview process. I will provide more information about this in due course, but for now know that it has been my absolute honour to serve you. I will continue to serve you in my new capacity as the Crone. My door will always remain open to you.'

I waited a beat but no applause followed. Tough crowd. 'All those who wish to say farewell to Hannah, please join us in the cremator room.' No one moved. 'Now,' I added firmly.

They started to move towards the door in a trickle at first, then in a wave. It was time for a eulogy for Hannah.

I hoped I could do her justice.

Chapter 25

Earlier on, Ethan had managed to contact Hannah's sister, Jennifer, and she had agreed to attend the Coven for the service. She stood next to the coffin, grief raw on her face. She had helped me write the eulogy so I could speak eloquently about Hannah's formative years and their time together in the Liverpool Coven before Hannah moved closer to their elderly father. He had died a long time ago but, having found her place in a Coven that had come to mean the world to her, Hannah had stayed

I managed to read those stories from her early life easily because I hadn't known her then. It was harder when I came to my part. I looked at Jennifer and spoke directly to her.

'Hannah was a very kind-hearted person. She had a strong work ethic and she never said no to anyone. As such, she always ended up working long days, but she rarely spoke a word of complaint. She was keen to help, to make the world a better place. She was ambitious, rightly so, and I saw her rising to the position of Coven Mother one day, either here or elsewhere. Her rune work was exemplary and her knowledge continued to grow as she studied in what little spare time she had. She was an asset to this Coven, not simply in terms of her skills and enthusiasm but also in her spirit.'

My eyes welled and I looked down at my papers, shuffling them to hide the moment of weakness. I waited until the lump in my throat had subsided before I continued.

'I selected her to help me guard her Coven sisters, Meredith and Ria, because I knew that she could be trusted. She gave her oath to assist me without hesitation. She was a witch of great heart, kindness and moral mettle. Her loss is a loss to all witchkind, but especially to this Coven and to her sister Jennifer, who has travelled from Liverpool to be with us today. Please close your eyes and join me in a prayer to the Goddess.'

I looked upwards. 'May the Goddess's eternal light guide Hannah's spirit on its journey. May she find peace and serenity in our Mother's divine embrace. As the stars do above us, may Hannah's spirit shine brightly in the realms beyond, a guiding light for those who follow in her path.'

My scalp prickled as I said the blessing of the stars and suddenly the pendant felt heavy around my neck. This blessing had once been said over my sisters and now they were guiding me. One day, I would guide the next Crone.

'Goddess, we thank you for the gift of Hannah's presence in our lives. May her memory forever be a source of inspiration and light. With heavy hearts, but filled with love, we bid farewell to Hannah Lions. With the Goddess's grace, so mote it be.'

'So mote it be,' the assembled witches responded.

I nodded to Ethan and he started the cremator. The coffin holding Hannah's body – I had double-checked – rolled into the fire.

My part was nearly done and I was grateful for that. Grief was resting heavily on my soul and my heart ached. We were gathered in the Coven common room and silence reigned once more. People stood in clusters, leaning on each other physically and emotionally.

I nodded at Oscar and he started 'The Parting Glass' playing through speakers placed around the room. The Celtic strains poured out, the soft drums echoing around the room and the lament swirled as the Coven's wizard guards moved through the gathered witches ceremoniously pouring a thimbleful of Farewell Elixir into each person's glass.

We stood and raised our glasses until everyone had a drink for a dearly departed guest and the last strains of the song faded into silence. 'Hannah Lions,' I said.

'Hannah Lions,' my Coven murmured back. As one, we drank our potion.

The elixir slid down my throat, warm and smooth. It selected one memory to show us of the person we were thinking of with our hearts and minds, one last memory of Hannah. I had expected it to show me one of the hundreds of times we had worked together but it showed me something else: a memory a couple of weeks old of something that had barely registered at the time.

Sarah had really turned a corner in her attitude, and I hadn't fully connected the dots. I'd thought her new, hard-working mindset was due to her demotion to acolyte; I'd even given myself a pat on the back for it. But it wasn't about that at all – it had been Hannah.

Sarah Bellington sat in the Coven common room, head thunking on the table. I grimaced and took a step forward to speak to her, but Hannah was closer.

'Contrary to popular opinion,' she teased Sarah lightly, 'it's not actually possible to knock some sense into yourself.'

Sarah sat up. 'I just don't get it. I swear I'm trying. I really do want to be a healer one day, but potion interactions are SO boring.'

'You can be anything you put your mind to,' Hannah replied. 'You're a bright girl but too often you cut corners. Witches can't cut corners, Sarah. Follow every step logically, and then you'll get the right result.'

Sarah huffed a little. 'Some days it doesn't feel worth the effort.'

'Only you can decide what effort you choose to put into your life. In your last days, will you be proud of yourself or not?'

Sarah rolled her eyes. 'Will you be?'

'Yes,' Hannah said without hesitation. 'I've always given life my all. And,' she paused dramatically, 'I am twice winner of the Cooper's Hill Cheese-Rolling Competition.'

Sarah sat up straight. 'No way!'

'Way,' Hannah confirmed. 'Even though I broke my arm once, I still won.'

Sarah broke into a huge grin. Hannah met my gaze across the room and gave me a small smile. I gave her a thumbs up and walked away.

As the memory cleared, I joined the circle of telling to share it, to share with her family and friends the positive impact she'd made with her life. A life cut too damned short but never wasted.

Chapter 26

I left the wake relatively early feeling bruised and raw. I started up to my apartment but Bastion tugged me further up the stairs. As he rarely called the shots, I let him lead me. 'Where are we going?' I asked.

'Out,' he responded shortly. He took me up to the roof terrace. 'I want to do something nice for you. Trust me?'

'Always.' The answer slipped out before my brain could censor it. His answering smile lifted the cloud from my heart a little.

Bastion shifted into griffin form. 'Climb on.'

'No harness?'

'We're not going far and you enjoy the extra thrill.'

He knew me so well – I did. I climbed on and made sure I had a firm grasp of the fur on his back. 'I'm ready.'

Without so much as a murmur of warning, he shot off. Barrelling forward with speed that ripped a surprised laugh from me, his wings snapped out and then we were flying.

He was right; we weren't going far. I watched curiously as he flew us over Lucy's mansion. There were wolves on the grounds, cavorting and tumbling together, but they didn't growl; things seemed friendly. Bastion did one last check, let out an eagle screech and then took us down to an open space just past the mansion. On the road at the end of the gated driveway, a horse and cart was waiting.

Not a horse. I blinked and stared more intently at the creature. It was a unicorn: Ares.

His white coat was marred by rippling scars and puckered flesh and his clawed feet were stamping the ground to signal he was getting bored with waiting. His red eyes flashed as he caught sight of us, and he threw his head back and gave us a magnificent whicker in greeting.

Bastion shifted to human form and we approached Ares together, hands interlocked. Bastion inclined his head. 'Thank you for agreeing to help,' he said to the unicorn. 'Lucy said you would be willing to assist us.'

Ares flared his nostrils and snorted at Bastion then turned to me and gently nuzzled me with his velvet-soft nose.

I smiled as his red eyes softened. 'Hello, Ares, how are you doing?' I checked him over. I'd performed some healing on him not so long ago, but his body showed no signs of his ordeal. His coat shone and he was nicely plump; Lucy had been taking excellent care of him. 'You're looking well,' I said approvingly.

Ares looked behind me. Bastion was already looking in that direction. I turned to see that a wolf was silently approaching, padding forwards, stalking us.

'Trying to sneak up on me?' Bastion asked, amused.

The wolf let out an annoyed chuffing sound. She shimmered and suddenly Lucy stood before us – buck naked.

She beamed at me, completely unselfconscious in a way that I could only dream of. 'Hey Amber! How are you?'

'I'm good, how are things with you, Your Majesty?'

She groaned. 'Don't you dare. If one more person "Your Majesty's" me, I'm going to punch their lights out.' A beat. 'Not their actual lights. It means I'll hit them,' she muttered to her wolf.

'It's good to see you,' the words slipped out before I could censor them.

'And you! We'll have to do some drinks soon.' She grimaced, 'I'm pretty swamped at the moment, but I swear, when Jess is back, I'll be carving time out for a girls night

out come hell or high water. There's some tequila with
our names on it.'

It was my turn to grimace. 'Champagne please, or at
least prosecco,' I protested lightly.

Lucy grinned, 'I'll happily buy you a porn star mar-
tini, and that's my final offer.'

'Deal,' I said, my heart feeling light.

There were some shouts behind us, and Lucy sighed.
'I'd better go. That was probably Greg realising that
I snuck off without a guard. Have a wonderful night
you two, don't worry about returning Ares and the carriage anytime soon – they won't turn into a pumpkin.'
With a wink, Lucy shimmered and in a moment she
was in wolf form. She turned on her tail and bounded
off lightly, crashing into the foliage with abandon now
that she wasn't trying to keep her position a secret.
I watched her go with a smile on my face; there was
something so exuberant about Lucy.

Ares nuzzled me once more, trying to get my attention back on him, then he turned and looked pointedly
at Bastion.

'I'm on it,' Bastion said mildly. He opened the door to
the black buggy. I'd never in my life ridden in an open-air
horse-drawn carriage before. Bastion held a hand out,

helped me in and I sat down on the red velvet seat. He sat next to me.

'Don't you need to drive?' I asked, a shade nervously.

'No, Ares will handle it,' he assured me. 'You just enjoy the ride.'

The air was a little nippy but it appeared that Bastion – or perhaps Lucy – had thought of that and there was a fluffy black blanket on the seat. Bastion laid it over my knees and I drew it up a little higher, running my hands over the sumptuous fabric. 'This is lovely,' I murmured.

'Almost perfect,' he agreed. 'Go on, Ares. We're ready.' Ares started to pull the cart, slowly at first with great prancing steps. 'Show pony,' Bastion snorted, though his voice was affectionate. 'A little faster Ares, if you will.'

Next he reached into the footwell where a cool-box was waiting and pulled out a bottle of champagne. He opened it easily and poured two glasses, all the while moving gently to the sway of the cart. He handed me the crystal flute. '*Now* it's perfect,' he said. He knew me better than to try and to get me drinking tequila.

Bastion tucked the champagne bottle back in the cool-box then put his free arm around me. I sipped the crisp champagne and let the bubbles burst on my tongue as I snuggled into him. The scent of him eased something inside me; he smelled of sandalwood and rosemary and something else that was uniquely him.

I gave a happy sound. Hannah's tragic death had reminded me sharply that life was too short. We needed to make the effort to enjoy every moment, and boy was I determined to enjoy this one.

Ares picked up his pace until we were moving at a pleasant speed. Snuggled in my blanket and wrapped in Bastion, I looked up and watched the night sky. The stars were twinkling overhead, bright and full of promise. I could still vividly recall wishing upon a star as a child, but in that moment I felt like I had everything I wanted.

'I love you,' I said to Bastion softly before I could stop myself. 'It snuck up on me, but there you go.'

He smiled. 'I love you too. It didn't sneak up on me,' he admitted with a wry smile. 'It struck me over the head and took me hostage.'

I laughed. 'I think that's the only thing that's ever taken you unawares.'

'Absolutely,' he agreed. 'Amber?'

'Yes?'

He took my glass and set it down in the drinks' holder. 'I love you,' he repeated sincerely, gazing into my eyes. 'With everything I am.'

'I know.' I smiled. 'I can feel it.'

He lowered his lips to mine, at first a gentle brush and then a firmer press. I opened my lips to him and his tongue swept in, gaining ownership over my mouth as he had already gained ownership over my heart. Love swelled down our bond, so raw and strong that the word 'love' seemed inadequate.

I had fought this for so long, longer than I would admit even to myself. We had been through a crucible of fire that would have brought any two people closer together, but something far deeper had forged our bonds. This easy camaraderie, the blending of our two souls – it was nothing like I had imagined love to be.

I had thought it would burn and be all-consuming like the juvenile love that had burned between me and Jake, and to a degree it did, but what was between Bastion and I was more than that. It was in every glance, every touch. Though we were together every moment of every day, I had never grown tired of his presence. He centred me in a way I hadn't known was missing from my life. He let me cry, made me laugh, and with him I could just be myself – every grumpy inch of it.

I realised I was crying. Bastion swept the tears from my cheeks with his thumbs. 'Hey,' he murmured with concern. 'You're crying, Bambi.'

'Happy tears,' I managed. 'I never dreamed of loving someone like I love you.'

As I pawed at my own cheeks, a sudden thought came to me. Some people still thought that Bastion was a *creature*, to be tagged or even killed. They believed he had fewer rights than them. My mind boggled at that; he was the best person I knew, and some people thought he was no better than an animal.

I curled my fingers around his neck and pulled him to my lips again, kissing him fervently as I silently vowed that the evil witches weren't the only ones I would take down. The Ante-Crea had better tremble in their bigoted boots because I was coming for them too.

Chapter 27

Like most things, education begins at home, so the next morning, I got up and tracked down Benji and, more importantly, Benjamin. They were in Oscar's flat, having a subdued breakfast. 'Are you okay?' I asked my dad, when I saw the slight shake of his hands.

'I had one too many drinks last night,' he admitted.

'Even after Edward spiked you?' I said incredulously. 'Are you crazy?'

'I brought up a bottle of whisky and I kept it stoppered and in sight at all times,' he reassured me.

'He did,' Benji confirmed. 'He even took it into the bathroom with him. I chose not to drink, Am. The memories are too fresh.'

'And imbibing alcohol also dulls the sense,' Benjamin pointed out primly.

'So you kept saying,' Oscar grouched, head in his hands.

'If you'd drunk less, my wizard friend, your head would not feel quite so awful,' Benjamin observed.

'Yes, thank you, Benjamin.' Oscar's tone was *not* thankful.

I turned my attention to Benjamin. 'We need to talk privately.'

One eyebrow rose. 'Right now, Miss Amber?'

Oscar's flat was far smaller than mine: a small, open-living space with a kitchenette-diner, one bedroom and bathroom. If I wanted privacy, we didn't have too many options. 'Yes, right now. We're borrowing your bedroom,' I said to Oscar. He nodded, head still in his hands.

'Where's David?' I asked as we went into the bedroom.

'He is returning to Edinburgh this morning. He was feeling anxious about leaving the Coven Council without a golem. He was also very excited to take a train. Ethan drove him to the station,' Benji explained.

I shut the door behind us. 'Sit.' I gestured to the edge of the bed.

Benjamin sat on the rumpled bed with a moue of distaste.

'We need to talk about your Anti-Crea beliefs,' I started firmly. 'I cannot tell you what to think, but I can tell you what actions will not be tolerated. Whilst I appreciate that you were made in a far different time—'

Benjamin held up a hand. 'Please stop there, Miss Amber. This lecture, though no doubt kindly intended, is wholly superfluous.'

'Superfluous? I don't think so! Conversations about bigoted beliefs are never superfluous. We are all guilty of cultural microaggressions now and again, but we have to consciously overcome those through deliberate action and thought. I—'

'Miss Amber,' Benjamin interrupted me firmly. 'The lecture is not superfluous because it is not a worthwhile topic, but simply because I have already seen past my previous state of ignorance. I no longer believe or support the theory that magical creatures have less worth than their purely human counterparts.'

Now I was stumped. 'Oh,' I said as the wind was thoroughly sucked out of my sails. 'What brought that on?'

'Benji is defined as a creature,' Benjamin said slowly. 'As I reside in his body that makes me one too, and I have never been into self-loathing. But honestly? It was the first time in his flesh that did it. I watched all Benji did and – forgive me, my friend – I could even hear his thoughts. They are pure. He is the kindest, most genuine being I have ever met. He is far greater than me. Bound now as we are, I fear the effect my thoughts will have on *him*.'

'I've told you,' Benji rumbled, 'you mustn't worry about that. Our thoughts are meant to be private. I don't blame you one bit for what you think – I only measure you by what you say and do.'

'And how do you find my measure now?' Benjamin asked curiously.

'So far I believe you have been in a difficult situation, forced to help others and to barter with their very life force to survive. Sometimes circumstances force us to make choices we wouldn't usually make. But you're not in that position any longer. Now you can make your own choices. Time will show what those will be, but there is no judgement from me for the choices you had to make before.'

'He helped Mum bind her mind and soul to an evil crystal of death,' I grumbled.

'Miss Amber, that was at your mother's insistence,' Benjamin interjected. 'I told her clear as day that she should seek another option. But time was pressing, so she did not.'

'So that was not his fault,' Benji added.

I blew out a sigh. 'No, it wasn't.' In her prime, Mum had been a force to reckon with; trying to tell her no was like trying to make the sun rise at night. 'Okay, well – good chat,' I finished lamely. 'Let's go and see what the boys are up to.'

I walked back into Oscar's cosy living room and paused. The atmosphere was tense. 'What's up?' I looked between Oscar and Bastion but neither man would meet my gaze. 'Well?' I asked impatiently. 'What is going on?'

Bastion finally turned to me. 'After we cracked the CD, I copied it and sent it to Incognito.'

'Your hacker friend?'

'My hacker *acquaintance*,' Bastion corrected.

'Okay. And?'

'And he just rang. He followed a paper trail for Shaun Bolton. A couple of years after your mum kicked him out, he used a few different identities. He was Grant for a while, then Toby. Then he went to meet with a high-end plastic surgeon and a low-end document forger.'

I swallowed. 'Does Inc know what Shaun looks like now? What name he uses at the moment?'

Oscar stood and put an arm around me. He led me to his sofa. 'Sit,' he urged.

I sat.

Chapter 28

'Just tell me,' I demanded tightly. My phone chose to ring at that moment. For once, I swiped to deny the call and send it back to the Coven reception so it could be re-routed for someone else to deal with. I put the phone on do-not-disturb mode.

Bastion sat on the other side of me and took my hand. 'John Melton.'

My vision tunnelled and I bent forward so that my head was on my knees. Bastion placed his hand on the back of my neck. 'Push against my hand,' he instructed quietly, 'and breathe.'

Easier said than done. My father, the man I thought had abandoned me as a child, had built himself a new name and a new face and ensconced himself in *my* Coven. He had never left me.

I felt utterly conflicted. John...? Spice Shoppe John? My mind couldn't comprehend it. But now that I knew, I wondered if I could see the traces of Shaun in him: the red hair, certainly and the shape of his eyes. I thought about his voice, the voice I'd known as Shaun's and now knew as John's. John was urbane and civilised, like Miss Doolittle to Shaun's Eliza. Shaun had transformed himself in more ways than his appearance; even the timbre of his voice was different.

Goddess protect me, I felt such a fool.

I realised I was shaking. My father had been running the evil Coven from *my* Coven. He had made a mockery out of me. Perhaps it was because he had wanted to see me grow up or, more cynically, because he needed to stay close to the harkan. I didn't know what to believe.

John – *Shaun* – had been furious when I was attacked by a fire elemental, though he'd seemed wholly uninterested in Oscar's injuries. It must have been difficult for him to see me day in, day out with Oscar, the man who had raised me and taken his own place in Mum's heart. No wonder he hadn't been crying a river for Oscar's wounds.

I wondered if Jeb had known. The evil Coven's organisation was cell-like and most evil witches didn't know many of the others. Had Jeb been ignorant of the true identity of John Melton?

And John – *Shaun* – knew my love of potions. Mum had introduced me to the Other realm when I was six years old and from that moment I had been obsessed with them. The DeLea potion bible had been the source of my bed-time stories more times than I could count. John had taken over running the Spice Shoppe no doubt as a way to get a hold of dark potion ingredients without raising eyebrows – and perhaps to have all those many, many run-ins with me.

John was always in the shop when I went there. Was he there to keep tabs on my movements? I felt sick as I wondered if Old Man Jones had died naturally or been helped on his way.

Through all the overwhelming turmoil, one thing an-chored me: Bastion. He was sending me waves of love, cocooning me. I closed my eyes and breathed through it all.

The prophecy!

I was supposed to face Shaun to bring an end to his rule of the evil Coven, but I couldn't for the life of me imagine hurting my father. That thought had been easier when I'd believed he'd deserted me without a backwards glance, but knowing he'd been part of my Coven for years changed that.

'I don't want to hurt him,' I said finally. I opened my eyes and looked at Oscar and Bastion. 'We'll hand him over to the Connection.'

Oscar's jaw worked. 'He's done very bad things, Amber.'

Benjamin huffed quietly. 'I'll say.'

'I know.' I held a hand up to forestall Oscar as he opened his mouth to argue with me. 'I'm not an idiot. You don't get to be the leader of a deadly organisation without getting your hands – and your soul – dirty. But he's still my father and I can't get past that. I want you two to know that I want him to get out of this alive – in a cell, but alive. Can we please aim for that?'

Bastion nodded. 'As long as it doesn't directly interfere with protecting you or risk someone else's life, I'll agree to it.'

I blew out a harsh breath. 'Thank you.' I turned to Oscar. 'And you?'

He nodded tightly but didn't give me his word out loud. I didn't ask again; I was probably already pressing my luck.

'What do we do now?' Benji asked. I met his eyes and he held out his arms to me. I went into them for the hug. I let his cold arms settle around me and it helped cool the tempest within me.

'We confront him,' I mumbled into Benji's shoulder. 'And we capture him.'

Chapter 29

My phone rang again. This time it was the Coven reception number and I grimaced. Someone was really trying to get hold of me. I swiped to answer. 'Crone.'

'Coven Mother,' Janice said briskly, 'I am sorry to interrupt. I am aware you do not wish to be disturbed but I have a lady on the phone who insists on speaking to you. She says her name is Charlize and she is your mum's carer. She says it is urgent.'

I went cold. 'Put her through,' I ordered brusquely. Janice didn't waste time. The phone line clicked. 'Charlize?'

'You need to get here now! We've been discovered. Someone's watching the house.' She sounded frantic and hung up before I could reply.

I swore loudly. 'That was Charlize – she said the location is compromised! Hurry!'

We all ran to the underground carpark. 'I'll drive,' I asserted, holding my hands out for the keys. Oscar had been drinking and he certainly wasn't at his sharpest – something I had no doubt he regretted now.

He hesitated before handing them over. He'd been steaming the night before, and most drunk driving was done the next morning when you felt deceptively fine but you absolutely weren't. He knew that as well as I did.

Bastion sat next to me, with Oscar and Benji in the back. I started the engine, threw the car into reverse and drove out of the car park. Next to me, I felt a buzz of disquiet from Bastion. He was looking at his phone. 'What's up?' I asked, keeping my eyes on the road.

'She didn't ring *me*.' His tone was a little hurt.

'What?'

'Charlize. She didn't ring me.'

'It's my mum that's under threat,' I rationalised. 'She probably had me on her brain.'

'Maybe,' he conceded, but the disquiet I felt from him didn't fade.

I didn't have time to pander to his hurt emotions because I was pretty sure that we were being followed and had been since we left the car park. 'Black Range Rover,' I said tightly. 'It's been on our six since we left.'

'Yes,' Bastion agreed. 'And so has the maroon Volvo behind it.'

Dammit, I hadn't made the Volvo. My fingers tightened on the steering wheel. 'What do I do? We don't have time for evasive manoeuvres.'

'Unless we want to bring more enemies to your mum's door, that's exactly what we do,' Bastion disagreed.

'Hang a left here,' Oscar instructed from behind me. I did, and both cars behind us followed. 'Take another left.' I took the left. 'There are lights up ahead. They're already on green so slow right down,' he ordered.

I slowed and ambled towards the lights.

'Orange lights, hit it!' Oscar barked.

I floored the accelerator and the car leapt forward just as the light turned red. I checked my rear-view mirror: the Range Rover had followed me and run the red light, but the maroon car hadn't. Maybe its driver already had points on his licence and couldn't afford any more, or maybe he didn't want to risk a collision with oncoming traffic. Either one worked for me.

One down, one to go.

'Speed up and then hang a right,' Oscar said. 'There's a road immediately to your left. Take it, then park the car on the side of the road. Benji, as soon as we hit the left, duck down.'

I sped up again, creating a little space between us and the car behind. It followed confidently and allowed a little more distance to creep between us. I took full advantage of that and floored it, breaking the speed limit more than a little. Then I careened around the corner and did a hand-brake turn into the left-hand road. I drove down a little way, slammed on the brakes and parked.

Oscar and Benji ducked low as Bastion pulled me from my seat onto his lap. Before I could object, he kissed me firmly, melting my bones and short-circuiting my brain. My brain restarted as he gently ended the kiss and deposited me back in the driver's seat. 'Drive,' he instructed.

I blinked rapidly. I looked around but there was no sign of the Range Rover.

'They sailed right past us,' Oscar said smugly. 'Now, get us to Luna!'

I started the car and we roared off. I prayed we'd get there in time.

Chapter 30

Mum's safe house was eerily quiet. There were no inter-lopers to be seen. 'What's going on?' I asked, confused.

Bastion frowned. 'I don't know. Wait for me to cover you before you get out. Keep your eyes peeled,' he barked.

His hands shifted into claws. Oscar had his lighter open and flicked, a small flame dancing on it. Benji's hands were clenching and unclenching as he looked around uneasily. He might not feel happy, but I'd once seen him take on a murderous ogre and win, so my money was on him. He'd been built specifically as a final defence for the Coven Council; there weren't many things he couldn't defeat.

Bastion slid out of the car and came round to open my door, covering me with his body. I got out, looking around a shade wildly. My heart was hammering. The tension was unreal. It felt like we were in the eye of the storm, waiting for the lightning to strike.

I felt rather than saw Fehu arrive. He gave a cautious *kraa* as he swooped the air above us.

'This doesn't feel good,' Benji murmured.

'It's not,' I agreed. 'It's a trap.' It felt a little better to verbalise my fears.

'A trap?' Benji paled.

'Well, it's not as much of a trap now that we *know* it's a trap,' I conceded, not letting my inner apprehension show.

'What do we do?' Benji asked, suddenly nervous.

'We spring it,' Bastion said grimly. 'Let's walk to the house. Cover Amber's back.'

Benji moved behind me obligingly as we walked to the house. Nothing happened. No attack. Nothing. The hairs on the back of my neck prickled.

I knocked on the door and Charlize opened the door with a smile. 'Hi! What a nice surprise. Come on in.'

Bastion's jaw tightened. 'You didn't ring the Coven and ask Amber to come here?'

'No.' Charlize looked at our faces and swore as she connected the dots. We'd been sent here by a third party, which meant a third party knew the location of the safe house. 'Incoming!' She hollered a warning to the occupants of the house. 'Just like we practised! Go, go, go!'

My mum and Meredith ran towards the kitchen, Meredith dragging Ria behind her. 'I don't want to hide,' she complained sulkily. Meredith ignored her and tugged her forwards.

I gaped a little when Fido, Ria's familiar, hopped onto Lucille's back and Lucille raced the two of them to the kitchen. In the kitchen was a door to the cellar, which doubled as a safe room.

'We'll tell you when it's all clear,' Charlize promised.

'You had better, young lady,' my mother harped. 'I am no coward!'

'Of course not. You're our last line of defence,' Charlize said calmly and winked.

Mollified, my mother went down the steps into the hidden bunker with the other two witches and the familiars.

'Frogmatch!' I exclaimed as the little imp swung into the kitchen.

'Ellie! It's good to be seeing you! It's been so boring around here. Have you brought us a fight?'

I smiled. 'It does seem that way, but we'll see. Maybe we're all being paranoid.'

Charlize shook her head. 'It's not paranoia when—'

'—they really are out to get you,' I finished wryly.

'You got it!' She looked at Frogmatch. 'You joining the party?'

'You bet!' he grinned, his mouth full of terrifyingly pointy teeth.

Charlize closed and locked the door to the cellar. The clank as it shut felt ominous. 'Amber, illusion runes and any curses you feel comfortable putting on it, if you please.'

'Yes,' I agreed crisply, galvanised into action. I wrenched the tote around my body and pulled out various vials as I dug around for the illusion potion that was left over from when I'd had to pretend to be my mum.

'Benji!' I summoned the golem. 'I need you to imagine a wall here. Just a plain brick wall, the same as this.' I pointed to the other area of red brick in the kitchen.

'No problem, Am.'

'Thank you.' I started painting the runes on the wall, modifying them from a human depositor to an inanimate one. I wasn't turning some*one* into someone else, but some*thing* into something else.

When the complex runes were ready, I turned to Benji and painted an *uttrycksyn* so that the vision in his head would link with the runes I'd painted on the door. Then I painted on protective and defensive runes onto the door that was now hidden by the illusion. I added a layer of scorpion runes; I may be a good witch, but I'd do just about anything to keep my mum safe, not to mention Meredith and Ria.

The ground under my feet trembled, forcing me to pause in my runing.

'That bloody earth elemental,' Charlize bitched. 'He's not getting away this time. Haiku! With me! Apollinaire, guard the kitchen! Do *not* leave it!' A hulking blond man walked in and gave Charlize a nod and a slightly mocking salute.

Haiku and Charlize ran out. They must have distracted the earth elemental because almost immediately the trembling stopped. I hastily finished my runes and activated them, making them invisible at first glance.

I grabbed my potions and shoved them into my tote. 'Benji? Can you hide in the walls and guard our witches?' I asked. Not that I didn't trust Apollinaire, but I didn't know him from Adam.

Benji's chest puffed out with pride. 'Absolutely, Am Bam. I'll protect your mum with my life. I swear it.'

Impulsively, I touched my hand to my chest and gave him a little bow. When I raised my head, his eyes were wide and full of tears. He bowed back to me then disappeared into the walls.

With Frogmatch on my heels I ran towards the outside door to help Bastion and Oscar with whatever was coming for us.

I was nearly there when I heard Charlize's agonised scream.

Chapter 31

I raced out, my mind blank with no plan in mind. At the threshold, my mouth dropped open when I saw the beast in front of me.

A chimera. Oh shit – we were in trouble. The chimera was somehow genetically linked to the griffins; because of that, griffins had no immunity to her brand of purple fire, and her scorching burns couldn't be healed in a shift. That was evident from the blistered forepaw that Charlize was holding tightly to her body. Still in human form, Haiku had run to her side to check the extent of the damage.

The chimera roared and the building shook. She was a tri-beast and had three heads: a lion's in the centre, a goat's to the left and a snake's to the right. Goddess, I hated reptiles. As well as her three hulking heads, she had sharpened cloven hooves and a goat-like body with a lethal scaled tail that Emory would have been proud of.

She turned her heads towards Oscar and let out a burst of flame from her gigantic lion's maw. I wished Lucy was here to pipe her; perhaps she could have talked sense into the creature. Then again, perhaps not.

'Fuck!' Oscar swore. He dived to the ground and most of the flames passed over him, but a few stray ones licked at his shirt and set it on fire.

'Roll!' I screamed. As he rolled on the ground, the giant chimera thundered towards him.

Flames extinguished, Oscar got to his feet again. He pulled air around him, his greying hair caught in the blast, then he chucked the ball of air towards the chimera. It hit her full in the chest and she stumbled backwards, screaming in outrage. Her tail whipped around her, trying to strike at Oscar.

Bastion, now in griffin form, plunged towards the striking tail, his talons extended as he rent into the chimera's flesh. She bellowed again and blew great billows of deadly purple fire towards him. He rolled out of the way of the flames – but only just.

My heart clenched with fear. This was one of the few beasts that offered a true threat to Bastion. I palmed the small vial of final-defence potion that rested permanently in my left pocket. My potion bomb was in my right pocket, and I wouldn't have wanted to mix those up in the heat of the moment. Left pocket for healing, right pocket for harming.

Frogmatch gave a battle cry and ran into the melee, growing in size as he went. 'Come and get me, goaty!' he challenged. The chimera gave another scream of rage and turned her attention to the imp.

He was still not much taller than a metre. 'Oops,' Frogmatch muttered. 'A bit premature, that.' He threw a bawdy wink at me. 'It's the only thing I'm premature in, I promise.'

'Watch out!' I shouted at the now medium-sized imp. A ball of flames rolled towards him and my breath caught in my throat as they struck his small red body.

'Frogmatch!' I screamed. Bastion dived towards him, but I need not have worried. Frogmatch's red skin danced with purple flames but they didn't seem to affect him one whit. He was immune to her fire!

'Thank the Goddess,' I murmured in relief, leaning on the doorway.

A voice spoke next to me. 'You'll find that the Goddess has very little to do with it,' my father said drily. It was his voice as Shaun, not as John.

I whirled around but he wasn't there, not physically. It was another audio-astral projection. I resisted the urge to ask how it was done.

'Now Amber, we can do this the easy way, or the hard way,' his voice said calmly.

'Could you be any more clichéd?' I huffed at him.

He considered it. 'I could disfigure my face horribly and laugh like a maniac, if you prefer?' His tone was humorous.

I folded my arms; I didn't want to joke with my father whilst his minion was breathing fire at my friends and the man I loved. 'What do you want?' I snarled harshly.

'We need your help, Amber. We need the potion that you concocted for Lucille.'

I knew all about the plight of the evil witches' familiars and I might even have felt a shred of sympathy; after all, it wasn't the familiars' choice to be linked to a witch that had turned down the path of torture and death.

I hardened my heart; they had made their choices, and I wouldn't do anything to help evil witches that continued to hurt and kill. 'No,' I said simply. I wouldn't help them, even at the expense of their familiars. The familiars were a weak point, one I could use to put pressure on the witches and I wasn't giving away that advantage.

'I have another chimera,' Shaun said calmly. 'This one's mate. Oscar and Bastion may survive one, but they definitely won't survive two. Alternatively, you can come with me and I'll call off the chimera when we're a sufficient distance away. Everyone gets to live.'

My heart plummeted. Two chimeras! Goddess, Oscar and Bastion wouldn't survive that.

Even as Bastion was fighting, I saw him turn to check on me as he felt my fear. Seeing nothing and no one around me, he clearly assumed I was scared for him. He sent me a wave of reassurance and turned to battle the chimera again. I watched, heart in my throat, as deadly flame roared past him again. This time it was entirely too close for my liking.

'If you don't come with me,' Shaun said lightly, like we were discussing tea and cake, 'I'll tell her to stop playing nicely. You'll notice that the only one who's been hurt so far is Charlize. A little warning shot, so they know my chimera is serious. But if I tell her to pull out the stops, that all changes, Amber. I know you're fond of Bastion, so I'm trying to be nice here.'

'You're failing,' I said bluntly.

He laughed. 'Maybe so, my dear, maybe so. But whether I'm nice or not, you really don't have much choice, do you? We both know that you love Bastion. One word from me and we'll have another chimera here flame-grilling him.'

'You're supposed to offer me my heart's desire,' I bitched. 'That's what the bad guys do. They offer wealth or the power to resurrect a loved one. You're not doing very well.'

'You've already got your heart's desire, Amber. My daughter – the Crone! I'm ever so proud.'

'Fuck off,' I snarled. 'You have no right to be proud of me, John.' Dammit, I hadn't meant to let his current alias slip out, but my anger at his pride had made it fall from my lips.

There was a pause. 'Ah,' he said lightly, as if my knowing his new identity was of no importance. 'The beans have been spilled, have they? All the more reason to crack on. Tick-tock, Amber. What will you decide? A second chimera coming out to play, or are you coming with me?'

My jaw clenched. I hated the idea of co-operating with him, but I hated the idea of Bastion dying even more. 'Where do I go?' I asked tightly.

He didn't crow in triumph. 'Into the red car that is idling at the front of the house. Go quickly. We don't want Bastion noticing you've slipped away or I'll have to distract him.' The threat was clear. I took a step backwards towards the house.

I heard an angry *kraa*. I looked up and met Fehu's eyes. *Don't,* I pleaded with him. *Don't tell Bastion I'm going. I have to keep him safe. Don't tell him I'm leaving or my father will kill him.*

Fehu screamed in rage and I felt his anger like a hot blast across my skin. He hated not being able to help us both. *Please*, I whispered again. He had been Bastion's familiar for two centuries and mine for a hot minute, so I hoped he would want to protect him a shade more than me. *Please*, I entreated and felt his assent.

I reached into my left pocket and set my vial of final-defence on the ground. *Make sure he gets it.* I wasn't taking something so valuable into the arms of our enemies. On the black market that little vial would go for a hefty seven-figure price tag. I wasn't giving them revenue to buy more dark objects.

After a moment's hesitation, I left my athame there, too. My enemies weren't going to leave me armed, and I didn't want to give them my family heirloom. I had my potion bomb in my right pocket. Here's hoping my enemies overlooked it.

Intending to take it off, I touched the pendant around my neck but it wouldn't budge. No matter how I tugged at it, it wouldn't lift higher than my eyeline. I guessed it was coming with me.

Above me, Fehu let out another angry *kraa*. The furious raven turned back to the chimera, flying at her eyes, claws extended. 'Raven!' Bastion cried, horrified, 'Get back!'

Whilst my clever little familiar drew everyone's focus onto him, I slunk away to my own private doom.

Chapter 32

As promised, the maroon car was outside the safe house with the engine running. I recognised the driver but I kept a closely guarded lid on my anger. If Bastion felt any sort of strong emotion from me he'd come running – chimera or no – and that meant he'd turn his back on the deadly creature. I couldn't risk that, even with Frogmatch's helpful immunity coming into play.

I climbed into the back of the car. 'Hello, Mack,' I greeted the driver as neutrally as I could manage, as if his treachery were nothing to me. He didn't deserve for me to waste my emotions on him; he was a pawn, nothing more.

'Amber,' he sneered at me. 'Thank you for co-operating with the plan.'

I wanted to knock the damned smirk off his face. With real effort, I ignored him. 'So,' I said calmly as I buckled up my seatbelt – safety is always important, even during a kidnapping – 'you're not anti-black magic after all.'

He laughed. 'Where better to hide than as a fanatic of the weak little white witches?' he chortled.

He was right. Even after Tristan had been revealed as an evil witch, I still hadn't looked twice at Mack. I'd hated him, thought he was a prick, but I hadn't thought he was evil. He'd played the role so well. With hindsight, I should have looked harder at him after Tristan's attack. Hindsight is such a smug bitch.

I folded my arms like I was in a snit. He seemed to be in the mood to lord it over me and that meant I could use his ego to do some information gathering. 'Did you serve Hilary as well as Tristan?'

'Oh yes,' he confirmed. 'I truly was fond of her. My anger at her death was not faked, I assure you. I really did enjoy slamming you into that dank jail cell. I would have thrown a few jabs into your ribs, but your father was clear that would not be tolerated.' He met my eyes in the rear-view mirror. 'More's the pity.'

'I doubt he was happy with the whole thing,' I blustered.

'He had no issues with Tristan's plan. He wanted to put pressure on you. You don't know Daddy Dearest at all,' he taunted.

He wasn't wrong there, but I knew a little about John and a little about Shaun. There was bound to be a bit of truth in the memories that I had of the latter, though I was conscious that as a child I hadn't had an impartial view of my father. My memories may have been distorted or affected by my childish admiration of the man; children are rarely discerning judges of character. Regardless, I knew the man more than Mack thought I did, and I fully intended to use that to my advantage.

Mack continued, 'We're far enough away now that we don't need to worry about the griffin. Drink this.' He chucked a small potion vial at me.

I studied it, stalling for time. I unstoppered the vial and gave it a cautious sniff, dipped my little finger into it and tasted it. It was definitely a sedative potion, a strong one. The amount in the vial would put me out for a couple of hours at least. I dithered, not wanting to be unconscious at Mack's mercy.

I looked up as I heard a click and stared down the barrel of a gun.

'Drink it.' All traces of humour had gone from his voice. 'Or I'll start putting holes in you.'

I believed him. I was all out of options. With a grimace, I drank. I unwound the window and tossed the empty vial out of the window before the sedation could take hold of me.

Mack laughed aloud. 'Leaving breadcrumbs, Gretel? Don't worry, little girl, the griffin will find you. We'll make sure of that.' He winked at me in the rear-view mirror.

Despair rose in me just as the world slid away.

Chapter 33

I sat up and touched a hand gingerly to my aching head. It was pounding and I was more than a little woozy.

'Mack gave you too much potion.' Shaun sounded annoyed. 'I'll speak to him about that.' His voice was heavy with threat.

I ignored him; I didn't give a hoot what he did to Mack. I reached into the pockets of my skirts but wasn't surprised when my hands encountered nothing more than lint. They weren't stupid enough to leave me armed with a potion bomb. More's the pity.

I sat up. 'What should I call you?' I asked my father. 'Shaun or John?'

'Dad,' he growled.

'That's what I call Oscar,' I said deliberately. It was easier to think of him as John because he was wearing John's face, speaking with John's voice. That had been his name to me

DESTINY OF THE WITCH

for over a decade. It also helped me separate him in my head from anything paternal – but I couldn't afford to do that. He was my father; he was *Shaun*.

His top lip curled in a snarl when I spoke of Oscar. 'I should have hit him harder,' he muttered.

I stilled. 'That was you? During the elemental attack?'

'Obviously,' he drawled. 'How did you think he got hurt?'

'By the car when we slammed into it.'

'That was unfortunate.' Shaun frowned. '*You* weren't supposed to get hurt. Unity were supposed to scare you a little, that was all.' He sighed. 'Never trust hired help.'

'I would have expected your advice to simply be "never trust".'

He smiled humourlessly. 'If your associates fear you enough then you can trust them plenty.'

'And did you fear the last leader of the evil Coven before you took over?' I asked pointedly.

His smile widened. 'No. And what makes you think I harmed him? Maybe he died of natural causes.'

I studied my father. 'He didn't though, did he?'

'No. He didn't.' He stood abruptly. 'You know why you're here. Make the potion for healing familiars and then we'll talk some more.'

'Bastion and the others – you called off the chimera?'
I didn't know why I was asking; it wasn't like I expected
whatever fell out of his mouth to be the truth – and yet a
small part of me still hoped it would be.

'They're all fine,' he murmured. 'Even your mother.'

'Leave Mum out of this,' I snarled.

'You're asking the impossible, my dear. She's as em-
broiled in this as it is possible to be. She is, as they say,
in the thick of it.' His voice was grim. He gestured to the
mass of potion ingredients lining the walls. 'You have all
the ingredients you'll need.'

'And how do you know what ingredients I'll need?' I
asked flatly.

'I catalogued the ones in your lab and in the Coven's
potion store and reviewed all your recent purchases at The
Shoppe. You have everything you need,' he repeated with
certainty.

I folded my arms. 'I'll need my workbook.' Hopefully
he – or a lackey – would get caught in the Coven while
fetching it for me.

Shaun gave me an amused look, opened a desk drawer
and pulled out my work notes and the DeLea potion bible.
'I took the opportunity to take these into my custody
whilst Bastion and Oscar were occupied.' A frown crossed

his face. 'I couldn't find the bloody grimoire, though. You've hidden it well. I thought it would be in the safe.'

I kept my face neutral. 'I destroyed it.' Kind of.

He studied me, 'I don't believe you,' he said finally. 'You might not want to use it yourself, but you respect knowledge. You wouldn't destroy it.'

'It was running out of life energy,' I lied with an easy shrug. 'As I wasn't willing to give it mine, it was the kindest thing to do to put it out of its misery.'

'Maybe,' he said finally, 'but I don't think so. I think you're lying, daughter of mine. No matter.' He waved it away and his expression turned serious. 'Now, I am not a fool, whatever you think of me. I know you don't want to make this potion, so I need to persuade you to make it properly. No errors. It's important that you know that Apollinaire is one of mine.'

I tried not to react but I suspect I failed spectacularly. Of course *someone* had betrayed us or else the trap wouldn't have worked. Someone who knew where we were must have told my father the location.

I thought darkly of the mocking salute the blond man had given Charlize. Thank the Goddess I'd asked Benji to protect Mum too, or who knew what Apollinaire might have tried whilst the others were busy battling the chimera.

Even so, panic laced through me. Apollinaire was guarding my mum and he could easily kill her whilst Charlize and Haiku were canoodling.

My father watched that realisation spread across my face with a smug, satisfied smile. The implied threat was I had to make these potions or Mum was dead.

Bastard.

Chapter 34

I glared at Shaun but he continued to speak, unfazed by the anger that was pouring out of me. 'I have agents spread across the Other realm. It's not just witches who work for me, Amber, though I'm sure you guessed that when you saw Mack. The evil Coven doesn't call itself anything so crass, though we've all enjoyed your little re-brand. Evil witches sounds so much more powerful. We like that.'

Great, I'd given them a nickname that they liked.

'The evil Coven is more than just a collection of a few witches choosing the path of power. We are the powerful from *all* walks of life. We call ourselves the Domini.' He spoke the name with reverence.

I snorted. That was Latin for 'master'.

A smile touched my father's lips. 'Yes, a touch unimaginative, but it has been in use for centuries so we are stuck with it now.' The smile faded. 'Make the potion, Amber.

After all, we have you for the harkan now. Make the potion, or the Domini will kill your mother.'

I tried to rein in my rage. Did my father think me so obtuse that he needed to draw out his implied threat into simple black-and-white terms? I had fully understood his earlier attempts at intimidation; I didn't need him to spell it out further. 'And are the Domini the Ante-Crea?' I probed.

Shaun snorted. 'Hardly. The Domini accept all powerful members, creature or human. Sometimes the Domini's interests have aligned with Anti-Crea interests, but we are only occasional allies, if that. Nothing more.' He looked at me. 'I have no issue with your relationship with Bastion, if that is what you're getting at.'

It was not. I couldn't give two figs about his approval; I was just trying to dig for more information on the Domini. But I smiled like I was pleased that he wasn't an Anti-Crea bigot.

Best to turn this conversation back to the potion and not my relationship with Bastion or the threat to Mum. If I focused on the latter, my fear and rage would make me weak and I couldn't afford that right now.

'I need the blood of the familiars you want me to save,' I said briskly. 'The potion will be far more effective if it is keyed to each familiar. I can make a generic batch, but it won't work as well.'

My father smiled. 'Excellent. I will get samples of the blood of the familiars that are here, and we can supply the generic potion to the international witches. If they want the full remedy, they will have to earn it.' Wasn't my father a keeper? 'Get started Amber.' He walked to the door then turned back. 'And Amber?'

'Yes?'

'I'll have a potion mistress check your work hourly. No deviations from the book.' He tapped the workbook then let himself out.

I released a shaky breath and slumped back onto the bed. What a mess. I let myself have a moment of fear and apprehension then gave myself a mental slap. Bastion would find me.

Bastion.

I reached for the bond between us but there was nothing there. Panic filled me as I realised I couldn't feel him – worse, he couldn't feel me. Would he think that I was dead? Oh Goddess, poor Bastion. And if he thought I was dead, did that mean he wouldn't look for me? Was he grieving somewhere, plotting revenge? Mack had implied that they *wanted* Bastion to find me; was that because he enjoyed the image of Bastion finding my dead body, or had they set a trap for him if he came hunting?

I bit my lip and grasped the pentagram necklace at my throat. I needed allies. I held it tightly but nothing happened. I pulled it up to my eyeline so that I could see it; the pentagram was usually bright silver but now it was burnished and blackened. Somehow the evil Coven – the Domini – had neutralised my link to my sisters and the Goddess.

I truly was alone.

Chapter 35

My pity party lasted a good five minutes; there were tears and even some silent wailing into my pillow. Then I took a deep breath and started plotting. I hadn't become Coven Mother and Crone by letting adverse conditions define me. Heck, I hadn't had a familiar for much of my life and that hadn't stopped me from achieving success. I believed in myself, and I wasn't going to stop now. I had allies and they *were* coming to help me – but for now I would help myself.

I had no idea how many familiars I was supposed to save in the UK, but the number of blood vials would give me a pretty clear picture of how many evil witches I needed to find and root out. I suspected my father would withhold the treatment from some of the less-privileged few so it might not give me a total picture, but it would be more knowledge than I had now. I would brew their damned potions and, whilst I was brewing them, I would brew another one. A secret one.

I started preparing some ingredients. As I chopped them, my brain was free to think. I hadn't been kidnapped to prepare this potion, as my father would have me believe, but because I was the only one who could completely control the harkan crystal. Anyone could make this potion, including the pet potion mistress who would apparently be checking on me hourly.

My father had my notes – they were warded, obviously – but I had no doubt that some judicious use of some evil runes would reveal them. So, what was his motivation in having *me* make the potions? Perhaps he didn't trust his potion mistress. That was a distinct possibility but I couldn't help sensing there was another reason – one I was missing. Maybe he was just trying to get me to relax into my surroundings by making me do something routine, lull me into a false sense of security. That felt very possible. Well, I wouldn't be lulled.

A click from the lock was all the warning I got before the door banged open and a cloaked witch barged in. The seer-bespelled cloak hid her features, but I knew it was a woman because of her petite stature. I kept my face neutral.

DESTINY OF THE WITCH

She glanced at the ingredients I was preparing, then went to leave. 'Wait!' I said. 'How many cauldrons should I prepare?'

She exhaled sharply as if she were annoyed but came back into the room. She went to my notebook, picked up a pen and wrote down the number fifteen. Then she walked out, slamming the door behind her.

She was avoiding speaking to me, which suggested that I knew her. My stomach sank: I was pretty sure I did but I didn't want to show my hand like I had so foolishly with Shaun. I'd make damn sure to hold my tongue this time.

Fifteen potions meant I had fifteen evil witches to root out. The Goddess sure was planning on keeping me busy – and that was without even thinking about the Domini. *One thing at a time.*

I looked around my delightful holding cell. Thankfully there were windows, but only the thin one at the top opened. With the best will in the world, I wasn't crawling through that.

I opened it anyway to get some fresh air and ventilation for my brewing, and whilst I was opening it I peered out. I guessed that I was on the second floor; the ground was some distance away but not terrifyingly far. There were bushes surrounding the building, making it look well-cared for, and in the distance were rolling hills and lots of grassland.

I recognised the hills: we weren't far from Edinburgh. No wonder Mack had knocked me out for the journey; neither of us would have enjoyed a four-hour car journey together. It also meant that night was falling, which was handy. The other potion that I wanted to create had a far longer brewing time, so I would start it, pretend I needed to stop for the night, then continue to beaver away in secret.

Armed with my wits and a plan, I felt much better. It would take more than a kidnapping to get me down. I was going to make sure my father regretted the day he'd conceived me – if he didn't already.

Chapter 36

I set up seventeen cauldrons: fifteen potions to be keyed to specific familiars, one potion to remain generic, and the last for my secret potion. Rather than using the desk-mounted ones, I set up two rings of them on tripod stands. The outer ring had nine cauldrons, the inner one had eight. Madame X, as I had christened her, hopefully wouldn't think twice about that because inexperienced brewers often set up spare cauldrons in case something went wrong. Hopefully she would assume that I was feeling nervous and was making spare potions in case I screwed up. Then I just had to pray to the Goddess that she didn't check the wrong cauldron.

I set up my other potion closer to the window so any different fumes coming from it would quickly be whipped away by the cold air. I guess that I had about forty-five minutes before Madame X returned, so I hastily continued chopping.

When I heard the familiar snick of the key in the lock, I hastily covered a handful of prepared ingredients with my workbook and continued to mince some rhodiola, careful to remove all the yellow flowers into the waste pile.

Madame X came in, gave the room a cursory glance and left again. The tension in my shoulders eased; she was clearly anxious not to be in my presence for any longer than was strictly necessary. Presumably, in case I identified her. She was too late in that regard, but her nerves worked to my advantage. She wasn't stringent in her inspections. This was absolutely going to work.

Now that most of ingredients were prepped, I turned on the flames under all of the cauldrons and started to make the bases. I let myself get lost in the intricate ebb and flow of stirring, mixing and making. Even when I was kidnapped, potion brewing was my happy place.

The next time Madame X came in, I called out, 'I'll stop for the night now. I'm tired and I don't want to make mistakes. I'll put these in stasis and finish in the morning.'

She gave a sharp nod and left. I grinned and started painting stasis runes onto all of the cauldrons, bar the last one. On that one I painted the stasis runes onto the lid but didn't set it on top of the cauldron. It needed another hour of brewing time before I could turn off the flames even temporarily.

I heard the snick in the lock after half an hour and hastily put the lid over the cauldron, but I misaligned it so that the runes wouldn't activate. I turned the flames down low and hoped that my visitor would leave quickly.

In strolled my father carrying a tray with two plates of food and two glasses of red wine. My stomach let out an audible grumble: I was both starving and parched. He set the tray down on a small table in the corner of the room. 'Join me?' he asked expansively. Like I had a choice.

I sat and he passed me a plate of food: roast chicken with vegetables, gravy and Yorkshire puddings. It had been my favourite dinner as a child, and I suspected he was trying to curry favour with me by remembering that small detail.

I hesitated before eating the food. I'd been present at the soul auction and I'd seen the dark objects they'd sold there. Poisoning his daughter would be the least of my father's crimes, though I doubted he would do that until he got what he wanted from me.

He saw my hesitation. 'It's fine,' he reassured me. 'Here, have mine.' He swapped the plates.

I snorted. 'A clever man would put the poison in his own food because he would know that only a fool eats what he is given.'

'And you are no fool,' he murmured, eyes flashing with amusement. '*The Princess Bride*, Amber. Really?'

'Inconceivable,' I muttered back, a smile tugging at my lips. We'd watched the movie together countless times. When Jeb had broken the clearing and given me back my memories, it had made them sparkly and new. They weren't memories of events that had happened thirty years earlier made murky by the passage of time, but memories of moments that felt like they had happened yesterday. If I thought too much about them, it made my heart hurt.

I hesitated another moment and he sighed. The smile faded from his face. 'I have pet wizards. If I wanted to harm you, you'd already be hurt. If I wanted to kill you, you'd already be dead. If I wanted to compel you, you'd already be doing my bidding. If I wanted truth from you, I have a truth seeker. I don't want any of those things, Amber. I want us to have dinner. I promise the food is safe.'

'Ah well, since you promised,' I said drily. I tried to keep the shock off my face that he had a truth seeker. The only one I knew was Jinx, but there had been a pale, thin woman at the soul auction who had been confirming the truth of what we said when we introduced ourselves on arrival, even though we were standing on truth runes. If my father had a truth seeker, she could compel people to tell the truth and she could affect their emotions. *She could make me trust my father.* The thought chilled me.

In the end, hunger and thirst won. I believed him: if he wanted me harmed, dead or compelled, I would be. My father had even urged me to get away when the Connection had raided the auction. For whatever reason, he seemed to want me to work for him willingly.

The food tasted delicious, but it was a lead weight in my stomach. Was Bastion eating now? Did he think our silent bond meant that I was dead? Was he grieving whilst I was eating a roast dinner and drinking wine? The wine soured in my mouth.

'What's wrong?' my father asked, a shade irritably.

'Bastion must be so scared for me,' I admitted. 'I feel awful for him. I just... I need to know he's okay.' I met my father's eyes. 'He's my familiar and I can't feel him. Do you know how awful that is?' Tears welled in my eyes. 'I can't feel him.' My lip quivered.

My father studied me. 'He's your familiar?'

Oh shit.

Chapter 37

I had forgotten that few people knew that Bastion was my familiar. We had used it to our advantage to get me out of those spurious charges levelled by Tristan but we hadn't let it become common knowledge. And now I'd let the cat out of the bag, all because my dad had brought me food and quoted *The Princess Bride* with me.

I nodded.

My father's expression was inscrutable before he gave a small sigh. He rubbed a hand over his face, pulled out his phone, dialled a number and passed it to me. I listened to it ring. Finally it stopped ringing and there was silence.

I sniffed and wiped away my tears. 'You have terrible phone manners, Bastion.'

'Bambi,' he breathed.

'I'm okay. They've shut down our bond somehow. But I'm okay.'

'I thought—' His voice quivered.

Hot tears filled my eyes. 'I know. I'm sorry. I'm so sorry.'

'I'm coming for you,' he promised. 'I'll kill them all.'

I don't know what it said about me, but that made me smile. 'I love you.'

'I love you. Be strong. I'm coming,' he promised fiercely.

My father snagged the phone from me and disconnected. 'Now eat your greens,' he ordered firmly, like I was still seven years old.

I ate quickly, keeping a surreptitious eye on the one cauldron that was still simmering quietly. I needed to add the yarrow root in the next five minutes or the whole thing would be ruined before it even got started.

I pushed back my plate. 'Thank you for the food,' I said politely. 'It's been a trying day and I'm tired. Perhaps we could meet for breakfast or something.' I dangled the carrot before him: *look at all the willing cooperation you'll get if you just leave me alone now.*

He stood. 'Of course. You must be tired after all the excitement.'

Excitement? That's what we call kidnapping, is it? I kept the bitchy thought off my face with effort. 'Why can't I feel him? Bastion, I mean?'

'This cell is carefully runed. One of them is designed to disrupt the bond between a familiar and their witch to make the witch more malleable.'

Lovely. 'Thank you for telling me.'

'Of course.' He paused. 'I'm under no illusions that we can repair our relationship in a day, Amber. But you're my daughter and I love you. One day at a time.'

I sighed. 'And how do you propose we overcome our fundamental differences? At the core, we are polar opposites. You are an evil witch, Dad.' I gave him the paternal title to throw him another bone of hope.

He smiled a little. 'You used forbidden runes to save Jake, Amber. You're not so different from me.'

My heart hammered. 'How do you know about that?'

He looked amused. 'Did you really think that, as two twenty-one year olds, you and Jake escaped and evaded assassins all alone? That house you rented in Shropshire for a very cheap rate? You rented it from me, Amber.'

I went cold. He had been my puppet master for far longer than I'd known. My heart was hammering and my time was nearly up. He needed to go now or my potion would be ruined. I stood. 'I think you should leave. I need to absorb this.'

'Amber—'

'Please. Go.'

He sighed again. 'I didn't mean for this evening to end this way.' He gave me a rueful glance. 'Things never seem to go the way I think they should with you.' He stepped closer and kissed my forehead. 'Sleep well, Am. Sweet dreams.'

He had said those words to me hundreds of times, and tears pooled in my eyes as he shut the door behind him. Damn Jeb for breaking the clearing. Damn Shaun for these sweet memories crowding my head.

I was lost in a sea of memories – and for once I didn't have Bastion to cling to.

Chapter 38

I worked through the night, not daring to nap for even half an hour lest I fall into a deep sleep and miss the next stage in making the potion. By the time dawn broke, it was nearly complete. Exhausted, I put the lid on it and let the stasis runes do their job.

Then I tumbled onto the bed and was out like a light.

'Amber,' John's voice called. For a moment I was confused as to why the heck he was calling me Amber rather than Coven Mother, but then it all came rushing back. He was Shaun, my father.

I sat up too fast and bumped heads with him with a loud crack. 'Ouch! You have a hard head,' I complained, rubbing my forehead.

'So do you,' he groused, rubbing his own head. 'You were sleeping pretty heavily and I grew concerned.'

'It took a long time to fall asleep after our discussion,' I admitted. 'It felt like I was awake the whole night.'

He grimaced. 'I'm sorry for that. Come, I brought us breakfast.'

I swung my legs off the small bed and joined him at the table. He'd brought me a blueberry muffin and a cappuccino, while he had a cappuccino and a croissant. 'Thanks,' I managed to say. I didn't tell him that I missed Oscar's overnight oats and freshly squeezed orange juice.

'This is nice,' he said, as he slathered jam onto his pastry. 'I've missed spending time with you properly as your father.'

I shoved some blueberry muffin into my mouth to stop myself saying something stupid, like fatherhood is about more than simply being a meal provider. It's about showing up for all your child's special moments. He'd done none of that, though admittedly that was because my mum had taken that choice from him.

Shaun persisted in making small talk with me whilst I ate. I mumbled half-hearted responses until I felt like I could reasonably ask him to leave. 'I need to get these finished,' I said finally, gesturing to the cauldrons. 'Maybe this evening we can talk about Mum and the harkan.'

He gave a tight smile. 'A nice, light conversation for later, then,' he said a shade sarcastically, but he stood up, tidied our breakfast tray and carried out our plates, leaving me alone with my potions.

I turned to my secret one first. Whilst that started to cool, I completed the familiars' potions. I deliberately took my time; I wanted to finish right after nightfall so my escape attempt would stand a slightly better chance of success.

I got lunch and seven more check-ins with Madame X before everything was finished. The last time she came in, she was carrying fifteen vials of blood. She stayed this time and watched as I added the blood to the cauldrons and stirred them as they cooled. Silently, she helped me decant the potions into vials, marking them carefully with the name of each familiar. I tried to see the names but she pointedly shifted them around to hide what she'd written. She placed them into a large wooden crate, then turned to stare at me.

The tension between us grew, but I refused to break the silence first. She clearly had something on her mind; perhaps she suspected I knew who she was.

I was startled when she finally spoke. 'I called Bastion,' Beatrice Wraithborne said. 'I confirmed your location.'

'Why?'

Her cowl hid her features but I had no doubt she was scowling. 'The witch who was posing as Felix on the Coven Council saw me as a rival for the leader's affections. He sought to cause disruption once he was discovered, but he also took the opportunity to try and kill me with the potion bomb. You saved my life. I recognise and acknowledge the debt,' she said begrudgingly. 'I tried to assist you in Tristan's kangaroo trial, but you would have got out of that anyway so the debt was not paid. Now we're all square. The next time I see you, we're back on opposite sides of the fence.'

'And your position on the Council?' I asked drily.

She shrugged. 'I will tell the leader that you recognised me. It was always a risk.'

'I did recognise you,' I confirmed. 'Right away.'

Beatrice pulled back the cowl so I could see her features. She fixed me with a stare. 'You acknowledge and agree that the life debt I owe you is settled? That calling Bastion with your location expunges the debt?'

'I do. So mote it be.'

'So mote it be.' She resettled the cowl over her features, grabbed the crate and started towards the door. She paused before she walked out. 'Be careful with that potion bomb. You could level the whole building. And don't delay your escape attempt – I'll be taking these vials to the leader right away.' She stalked out and locked the door behind her.

Great. She hadn't been as unobservant as I'd thought; this whole time, she'd known full well I was brewing a vat of volatile potion bomb.

Chapter 39

I despise waste, but I couldn't possibly take all of the potion bomb I'd made with me. I decanted two dozen vials and put a dozen of them in my left pocket and a dozen of them in my right pocket. Then, with significant regret, I added arrowroot into the remaining potion to nullify it. What a damned shame.

Beatrice had told me she wouldn't give me much time, and Bastion was on his way, so I needed to act now. At the thought of Bastion, I reached inwards but he still wasn't there. As I looked, I suddenly saw that something else *was*. The ward runes may have been enough to disrupt one of my familiar bonds – but not enough to disrupt two.

My bond with Fehu was faint in comparison to the all-consuming roar of the one with Bastion, but it was there. I gave it a solid tug, and suddenly felt that he was much closer. That comforted me, though I had no idea what use the raven would be to me besides being able to lend me some extra strength.

I pulled one of the vials out of my pocket and stepped back. Historically, I had terrible aim. I pulled my magic through the vial to activate it, then hauled my arm back and threw the vial at the base of the wall opposite me. Naturally, I missed and struck the window instead. Glass shattered and sprayed everywhere, and I covered my face as stray shards blew back at me. I felt several stings as some of it cut me, but it couldn't be helped.

I had created a significant hole in the wall. It was too high for me to jump through easily but I had plenty of firepower. I threw another vial at the wall to make the hole bigger and there was a rumble and another boom as the potion bomb struck the wall. The bricks and masonry dust sprayed outwards this time and my escape attempt was definitely noticed. I heard shouting.

I had been planning on lowering myself so that there wasn't too much distance to fall. Hopefully I'd land on the cushioning bushes below; at two floors up, I was going to break limbs but I wouldn't die unless I landed on my head – and I was hoping to avoid that. With the shouting, though, adrenaline surged through me. It was now or never, and there was no time to descend carefully.

I pulled on my bond to Fehu again, took a deep breath and *ran*. I leapt through the hole, arms and legs milling. *Don't hit your head!* I screamed to myself as I plummeted towards the ground. The fall was over in seconds – and before I could hit the ground with a crunch of bones, claws grabbed me, digging into my shoulders and lifting me up.

I cried out at the stab of pain and felt Fehu's distress. *Fehu?* I looked up to see my rescuer; I had been expecting to see Bastion, but instead I was looking up at a bundle of black feathers. 'How the heck are you carrying me?' I shouted at the small avian.

He ignored me and kept on flapping his wings purposefully, lifting us higher into the air. I was being lifted by a raven – a large raven, but even so it should have been physically impossible.

Magic, came the amused thought from the bird.

Well, yes. There was that.

Fehu lifted us higher and I tried not to look down. Now that I was out of the confines of the wards, my bond with Bastion slammed into me. He was almost incandescent with rage – and he was also very, very close.

'Can you put me down?' I shouted to Fehu, a shade panicky as my legs flailed reflexively. It felt like one wrong move and I would plummet to my death. I was fine flying on Bastion, but it was different being carried instead of riding. 'I really don't like that there's nothing between my legs!' I hollered.

'I'm always willing to be between your legs,' Bastion said as he flew up behind me. He nudged his head between my legs, moving carefully until my legs were astride his back.

'I've got her,' he said to Fehu. 'You can let her go, raven.'

Fehu gave a triumphant *kraa* and pulled his claws from my shoulders. I winced with pain and Bastion let out a shriek as he felt it. 'Let's get you healed,' he growled fiercely.

I leaned low on his back and hugged him fiercely, sending him a wave of love, relief and joy. His echoing joy bounced through me, but his anger was still simmering underneath. He would kill anyone who dared harm me.

He wheeled around and headed straight towards a clearing in the forest. The place was a hive of activity, and I gaped as I saw my mum imperiously ordering people about with not a trace of her usual forgetfulness fogging her eyes.

Bastion landed lightly and I scrambled off his back. 'Shift!' I demanded.

He shifted and I threw myself into his strong arms, pulling his head down for a fervent kiss. He responded just as passionately, holding me hard against his body. I felt his rush of desire. Luckily his need to see that I was safe dampened his ardour because otherwise I could feel that he'd have taken me there and then.

I pulled back, eyes wide. 'Not here!' I said scandalised.

He sent me a predatory grin. 'Not here,' he agreed. 'Soon,' he promised huskily. He kissed my lips lightly. 'You left these.' He passed over my athame and vial of final defence. 'Don't lose them again.'

'No, sir,' I quipped with a salute. I put the small vial in my left pocket and slid the athame back into my ankle holster.

Bastion tucked some stray hair around my ear. 'Let's get you fixed up.'

I kissed him gently one last time. I couldn't get enough of touching him. 'Hold that thought.' I looked behind him to the people in the clearing. One person stood out, of course. 'Mum?'

She turned and smiled at me, her eyes knowing. She looked at me and she *knew* me. 'Hello, Amber.'

Chapter 40

'Mum!' I ran to her. She was having a lucid day, thank the Goddess. She gathered me into her arms and squeezed me. I hissed a little as all my cuts and scrapes made themselves known. 'What are you doing here?' I asked.

'It calls to me,' she said faintly. 'The harkan.' She looked at me with haunted eyes. 'I had segregated my mind as much as possible to stop me falling under its thrall, but obviously it didn't work quite as I intended.'

Lucille was draped around her neck, deathly still. 'Lucille?' I asked fearfully. Maybe my potion hadn't worked after all.

'She's helping me,' Mum admitted. 'Without her, I wouldn't be here. Your potion worked. It rejuvenated her completely, and now she's giving me her all so we can finish this as we should have done years ago.'

'This isn't your fight,' I argued. 'Go home. Take Lucille. You'll both be safe.'

'No, we won't.'

I didn't argue with her because that was when I remembered something important. I turned to Bastion. 'My father said Apollinaire was one of his and that's how he knew our location.'

Bastion frowned before shaking his head. 'No,' he said finally. 'I know Apo. There is no way he would betray me.'

'Maybe he didn't see it as betraying *you*.' I pressed my lips together. 'I know this is hard, but—'

'No,' Bastion said, and sent me absolute certainty through our bond. His ability to read people was second to none.

I bit my lip, 'If it wasn't Apollinaire who betrayed us, then who did? Someone told my father Mum's location.'

Bastion shook his head. 'Not necessarily. We could have just missed a tail one time.'

'Do you believe that?'

'No,' he admitted. 'I don't.'

'Then what do we do? If we have a mole...' I trailed off and looked around us. I trusted them all. Charlize and Haiku were standing by Melrose, Meredith and Ria. Benji and Shirdal were talking to Apollinaire and Oscar. Frogmatch was sitting on Benji's shoulder. Ethan and Jacob were standing by Kass.

Kass caught sight of me and swung her blue backpack around to the front of her body as she came over. She rifled in her bag and pulled out potions and paintbrushes. 'Are you okay?' she asked, even as she started to paint healing runes on me.

I smiled. 'I'm good. I'm tired and my body aches. I guess I feel a bit like you on a bad day.' Now wasn't really the time – but we were about to wade into some sort of battle, so maybe it was. 'Listen, I've been working on a potion to help with your fibromyalgia but I haven't had time to finish it yet. I'm sorry.'

Kass startled me by pulling me into a hug. 'Where you find the time and energy to help so many, I'll never know. Thank you – thank you for thinking about me. It means the world that you'd even acknowledge what I'm dealing with, let alone try and help me manage it.' She cleared her throat. 'Luckily, today is a good day and I am ready to kick some evil-witch ass. You got any lying around?'

I grimaced and told her that Beatrice Wraithborne was Madame X.

'For fuck's sake,' Kass muttered. 'She was standoffish, but I thought she was one of the good ones.' She closed her eyes in despair. 'They're fucking everywhere.'

'They're not,' I reassured her. 'There's about fifteen in all of the UK Covens.'

'Fifteen is fifteen too many.'

'I hear you, but that's one bad witch in every two Covens. It's manageable.'

Shirdal swore. 'Car approaching!'

We all fell silent and looked in the direction he was watching intently. It took a few minutes for the vehicle to arrive. Behind the wheel was a wild-looking Willow. I had never seen the Coven councillor ever look less than serene, even when she'd hosted the Goddess herself in her body. Behind Willow were the witches I recognised as the Maiden and the Mother.

The Goddess had sent backup.

Chapter 41

'Crone.' Willow greeted me with a respectful bow.

'Willow, good to see you.' And it was. Willow had proved herself time and time again, not to mention she had hosted the Goddess herself in her own body. She was one of the few that *was* trustworthy; the others that were definitely trustworthy were the two Goddess-blessed in her car.

'You know the Mother, and the Maiden,' Willow introduced us.

'I do,' I confirmed, 'but loosely. Knowing your real names would help.'

'It is forbidden,' Willow chastened with a frown.

'More like not encouraged,' the Mother replied with a wink. 'I'm Justine, this is Kate,' she gestured to the Maiden. 'We've been sent to help.'

Kate was young and she was grinning at me with youthful vigour and excitement; she was riding into danger and excited about it. Oh, to be young and reckless again, when you thought you were immortal and nothing was to be feared. I was older and I knew plenty of things that would get me quaking in my boots, though facing my father wasn't one of them.

'I'm grateful for it.' I hooked my pendant out of my neckline. 'I don't suppose either of you can fix this?'

Willow let out a gasp. 'That is vile!' she gasped. 'They have defiled the sisterhood pendant with blood! It needs to be cleansed. I will start right away.'

I was fumbling with the clasp when strong hands rested on my shoulders. I stood still as Bastion carefully undid the necklace for me then held it out to Willow. Huh. When I'd tried to remove it before I'd let myself be taken it hadn't shifted, yet now it would come off. It was a fickle thing.

'Thank you,' Willow said politely as she took it from him. 'Crone, leave this with me. I'll have it singing with your sisters' souls in a few minutes,' she promised, grabbing a tote bag out of the car.

I turned to Kate and Justine. 'We haven't had much opportunity to work together yet, and this is rather throwing us in at the deep end, but is there anything I should know about the Triune? Anything helpful we can do?'

'We can link our power giving one of us the power of three,' Kate offered.

'That might be helpful,' I conceded.

'Why do you think we're here?' she said with a cheeky grin.

'And you'd just ...give me your power?' I asked.

'For however long you need it,' Justine confirmed. 'We're here to help you, but this is your show.'

'Think of us as your back-up singers,' Kate suggested.

Justine sent her a withering look and rolled her eyes. It made me smile; their friendship was clear to see, despite the age gap between them. 'We're not back-up singers, we're just *back up*.'

'You're the one who said it was her show!'

I cleared my throat, 'Well, thanks. I'll be sure to get your help when it's go time.'

'Good. In the meantime, have some ORAL potion.' Justine rooted around in her bag and passed me a vial. As Kate snickered at its name, I drank the potion and handed the empty vial back to Justine. 'Thanks. Are you both good?'

'We came via a portal,' Kate reassured me. 'We're fully charged and ready to go.'

'Great.'

I excused myself and went to speak to Shirdal. I needed some war counsel, and he was just the man to give it.

Chapter 42

'Shirdal,' I greeted him. 'Thank you for coming.'

'For you, sweetheart, I wouldn't be anywhere else. What's the plan?'

'I really don't know. To be honest, I was hoping you'd have a plan.'

'Killing everyone usually works,' he suggested with no trace of humour.

'Let's leave that as Plan B,' I suggested. 'There are definitely captives here – my father said he has a truth seeker held here.'

Shirdal's eyebrows shot up. 'Okay, rescue the seeker then kill everyone else.'

'Our priority has to be the harkan.'

'Which is?' he asked patiently.

'A deadly crystal of murderous power that is slowly eating at my mother's mind,' I said simply.

Shirdal nodded. 'It's on team evil. We'll kill it.'

I grimaced. 'I don't think it's that easy. It contains hundreds of people's life forces. It's not going to be easy to destroy.'

'Nothing worth having comes easy,' he shrugged. 'They won't be expecting us to return so quickly, so we have the element of surprise.'

I thought of Mack's throwaway comment. 'About that... I think they *are* expecting us. Mack said –'

'Mack?' Bastion interrupted with a furious growl.

'He was the one that took me from Mum's safe house,' I explained. 'He's working with the evil Coven and the Domini.'

'The Domini?' Bastion asked.

'An organisation that takes after *Pinky and the Brain*,' Shirdal replied. At our blank stares, he elaborated, 'They want to take over the world.' It figured that Shirdal would know something about the shady organisation.

Bastion fixed me with a stare. 'You'd best start at the beginning, Bambi.'

So I did. I told them everything, from my dad's audio-astral projection to our chats and my final escape. It had all been just a little too easy; combining that with Mack's comment made me think that they wanted us to come after them, which meant they'd be prepared for us. Though *why* they'd want that, I didn't know.

'They might be expecting us,' Shirdal conceded, 'but they don't know that we know that they're expecting us. So we still have the element of surprise.'

'I don't think we do.' I frowned. 'It may not be Apollinaire, but we have a spy in our midst.'

'All the more reason for you to stay with Charlize–' Bastion began.

'No,' I interrupted firmly. 'This is a family affair. I need to be here.'

'Amber...'

'No,' I repeated. 'So what's next? We can't take Ria with us, nor can we take Kate.' I didn't feel comfortable bringing teens into battle.

'If we don't, we'll have to leave men behind to guard them,' Bastion pointed out. 'We're already sparse on the ground. A few witches, a wizard, a handful of griffins... If we have to leave any of them behind, we're really spreading ourselves thin.'

'Let's leave Ria and Kate with Benji,' I suggested. 'He'll keep them safe. And we can see if Meredith or Melrose want in or not. Everyone else, with us.'

Bastion gave my shoulder a squeeze and went to speak to Meredith and Melrose.

Willow sauntered towards me with a triumphant grin on her face. 'All cleansed, Crone.' As I reached out to take the pendant from her, my eyes leached to white. My head flung upwards, fixing on the stars above.

The Goddess wrenched me from my body and showed me the future which might be.

Chapter 43

The Goddess showed me Justine and Kate staying behind in the car, unconscious as they sent their everything to help me, guarded by Benji and Ria. She showed me using the glowing white pendant to find where the harkan rested in a library. The crystal glowed malevolently in its box, pulsing with the desire to destroy but hampered by my mum and our bloodline. It needed a bond to be truly unleashed.

The vision shifted and the Goddess showed me Frog-match slipping silently into my skirt pocket, then she showed me Bastian and Shirdal fighting a chimera. She showed me the truth seeker crying in her cell and Benji pulling her through the walls. The Goddess imbued a sense of trust as I saw the truth seeker, for whatever reason, the Goddess wanted me to trust her. Finally, the Goddess showed me, *raising a blade high and sobbing as I brought it down.*

I jerked back to my body. Blinking rapidly, I cleared my eyes. Somehow, even though we'd left Benji guarding the others, he would make his way into the building. I grimaced. The vision had hardly been useful, apart from telling me we could trust the truth seeker, I didn't know what else I'd gleaned from it that we could use.

'All right, Bambi?' Bastion murmured, pulling me into his arms. 'You left us for a moment.'

'The Goddess sent me a vision, though I'm not sure why. It wasn't especially helpful. She agreed with us leaving Benji, Ria, the Mother and The Maiden behind though.'

'At least we know we're on the right track.'

'I guess. She showed me you and Shirdal battling the chimera, and Frogmatch hiding in my pocket for some reason. ' I rested my head against his chest as I struggled to understand what I'd seen. 'I really just want to go home and read a good book in the bath.'

Bastion's chest vibrated with silent laughter. 'Later, witch. I promise I'll give you your heart's desire as soon as we have vanquished some evil.'

I mock sighed. 'You always want to vanquish evil first. Your priorities are all wrong.'

'It will give me the opportunity to kick down some doors,' he teased. 'You always enjoy that.'

My skin warmed; something must be wrong with me because I really did enjoy watching him do that. He'd once pulled an evil witch's curse down on himself by trying to impress me by kicking a door down. At the time I hadn't been impressed, but now that he was *mine* something about the raw display of strength made my knees go weak. Though watching him do dishes still topped the list.

'Goddess help me but I do,' I admitted.

That made him laugh again. 'Was that so hard to admit?'

'Yes.'

He grinned. 'Come on, let's go and spring a trap.'

'I wish you didn't sound so excited,' I muttered. 'Last time we sprung a trap, there was a chimera and I got kidnapped.'

'And there'll be a chimera this time, too. The difference is that this time we know to expect it and we won't be on the back foot.' He fixed me with a hard look. 'I'm loath to be separated from you after we've already been apart for so long, but I'd rather you were far away from the chimera. You'll have Oscar and Frogmatch guarding you, and your athame and a tonne of potion bombs. And this time, you're not ditching your guards, are you?'

'Nope. No ditching here. I'll be super good,' I promised.

'You'd better be or we'll be talking about it later,' he growled at me. Then he leaned forward and kissed me until I couldn't see straight.

I hated that it tasted a little like a farewell.

The witches were an essential part of the frontal assault. We crept forward, paintbrushes at the ready. When we touched the walls, the wards lit up like a Christmas tree at a shopping centre. With Ethan and Jacob to my right and Meredith and Melrose to my left, we all started painting cancelling runes.

'There are scorpion runes!' I hissed a warning to the others. 'Be careful!' I painted quickly, deactivating the murderous wards hidden among the innocuous ones. Kate and Justine had given me their magical power and energy and I felt like a three-year-old who'd eaten a bag of candyfloss and then downed an espresso coffee. I was so hyped up it was hard to contain my energy. I painted with a speed and efficacy I had never dreamed of acquiring.

When both teams told me that they were ready, I pulled down the wards. Bastion could have coaxed them down, but he had reluctantly admitted that pulling down that volume of runes would have left him tired and weakened. I wanted him to be neither of those things if he might be facing a chimera again.

With the wards down, Bastion kicked down the door with his black military boots. My insides warmed. Man, I really did love it when he did that.

'Spread out,' Shirdal instructed. 'Find the truth seeker or the harkan.'

A scream that was both a sibilant hiss and a roar rang out. 'The chimera is here,' Oscar grimaced.

'We're ready for her,' Bastion said grimly. 'Stick to the plan.'

I pulled out my pendant. 'Show me the way to the harkan,' I instructed it. It rose from my chest and pulled me forward. I let the magic guide me, with Oscar and Mum following close behind.

My sister-blessed pendant tugged me towards a set of mahogany doors that I recognised from the vision. *This way, Princess,* Abigay's voice whispered in the chambers of my mind. *Be on your guard,* she warned.

The pendant pulled me towards the library I'd seen in the Goddess's vision, but before I could open the door Ria came running down the corridor.

'Ria?' I asked in confusion. What was she doing here? She was supposed to be with Benji! 'What the heck happened?' I demanded.

'We got attacked! Benji's hurt! Hurry!'

Dammit, not again! 'You stay here,' I ordered Oscar and Mum. 'Find the harkan. We'll get Benji and join you.'

'We shouldn't split up,' Oscar argued.

'I have Frogmatch. Just find the damned crystal!' I barked. The imp was in one of my pockets, waiting like a live grenade. 'I'll just be a moment,' I promised.

'This way!' Ria shouted urgently as she ran further down the corridor, looking back urgently at me.

'I'm coming! Lead the way.'

Ria moved back the way she must have come and led us through a series of winding corridors before finally arriving at another door. We followed her in. The large room contained only a few rickety looking wooden chairs, a host of dark shadows – and an unconscious Benji slumped on the hard wooden floor.

As I crossed the threshold, wards snapped into place, snaring us in the room.

Damn it.

Chapter 44

A low hiss and a growl from the deep shadows suggested that we had found the second chimera that my father had bragged about. I ignored it and ran over to Benji. 'Benji!' I shouted as I knelt by him. 'Benji?' I lifted his head onto my lap.

'I deactivated him,' Ria said smugly.

My mind went blank. 'Why would you do that?'

'Dad wants you most of all,' she said, her voice petulant. 'He wants you in the library, to bond with the harkan, but I'm going to kill you and take your place. *I* should have all that power, not you. You're pathetic.'

'Dad?' I said feebly, my mind failing to connect the dots as I stared in horror at her.

She grinned at me but there was no warmth in it. 'Oh yes, *Coven Mother*,' she sneered. 'All this time, you and I have been half-sisters. When your father got divorced from your mum, he took up another identity. Grant Plath. *My* father.'

Everything fell into place. After he'd been Shaun, he'd been Grant and then Toby before he'd become John. I looked in horror at Ria, who was still continuing her triumphant monologue.

'When he'd had enough, he ditched Meredith but he never left *me*. He got a new identity and he joined me in the Coven as John. He cautioned me to hide the true strength of my magic and taught me to stay under the radar. He had me break the wings of that bird and let it go, just so you could find out about me and I could act all contrite. I did a great job, didn't I?' She laughed with delight, clapping her hands childishly.

'You believed me, hook line and sinker. "Oh I never meant to be an evil witch, they led me astray!"' She snorted. 'As if. I begged Dad to let me do more and more. Runing that griffin bitch, feeding off her fear and then her thirst and starvation – it was delicious. I was full of power for days.'

She laughed. 'And then Edward came to help get me out of the circus because, honestly, I was just so bored. Of course, I could have got myself out if Meredith hadn't confiscated my damned phone,' she grumbled.

'Edward nearly killed your mother!'

'I know – such a pain that he didn't do a better job. I was going to smother her and finish her off, but Cain wouldn't leave my side.' She grimaced. 'I might have overdone the distraught teen a bit too much. Ah well, live and learn.'

'You're psychotic.'

'Runes and stones may break my bones, but words will never harm me,' she sang. 'Listen to us, bickering like real sisters!' She winked at me. 'Anyway, Edward and I were going to kill you when you were "rescuing" me from the circus, but you and Bastion flew instead of getting in the car with me, which really ruined my plans. I had to call Edward off.' Her voice became petulant.

The chimera let out another rumbling roar. 'Not yet,' Ria huffed at it. 'Settle down.'

It ignored her and stalked forward, all three sets of its eyes glaring at me. I carefully laid Benji's head on the ground, frowning a little as it moved easily again. When Benji was deactivated, he became immovable like solid rock.

I didn't have time to ponder that any further. I scrambled to my feet and pulled two things out of my pocket: one was Frogmatch; the other was a potion bomb.

'It's go time, Ellie!' Frogmatch howled happily. He swung down from my hand and started to grow in size. 'Distract the chimera fucker till I'm bigger,' he said to me. He glared at Ria. 'And you – you'll get your comeuppance, young lady. I *protected* you.'

Ria rolled her eyes. 'I'm shaking in my boots. Oh no! An imp is going to get me.' She laughed loudly.

Clearly, she hadn't seen an imp at their full size. I was almost looking forward to this. Every day was a school day, and Ria was about to learn one heck of a lesson.

Chapter 45

Frogmatch grinned at Ria and flashed his needle-like teeth as he started to grow in size. I didn't allow myself to be distracted by them; my focus was on the huge chimera slinking forward with her eyes fixed on me.

I threw a potion bomb, aiming it at her feet to scare her back. Naturally I missed and struck her full in the chest. The blast sent her rocketing back and she let out a yowl of fury.

Behind Ria, Benji sat up. He grabbed the nearest wooden chair and smashed it over her head. Ria went down like a sack of potatoes.

Frogmatch sighed. 'I wanted to do that,' he complained to Benji. 'I had my eye on that chair.'

'Why, Mr Frogmatch, I do apologise,' Benjamin drawled. 'But I have very limited experience in such mat-

DESTINY OF THE WITCH

ters and I did not want to leave that young lady as a threat for much longer.'

'Benji?' I asked urgently.

'I was able to protect him from the full hit of the de-activation *ezro,* Miss Amber, but it has knocked him unconscious for the moment. I have been shouting and hollering at him something fierce, and he is certainly coming around. I believe he'll wake imminently.'

Benjamin paused. 'In truth, I was hoping he would wake up so he could attack Ria for us. In the meantime I played possum, but I saw the opportunity and I knew I had to seize it.' He flashed an uncharacteristic grin. 'I find I now understand a little more about the human pre-occupation with violence. Boxing now makes some sense to me. It is rather fun.'

'I'm glad you're enjoying it,' I said drily. 'Can we focus? Can you help Frogmatch fight the chimera whilst I get us out of these warding runes that are locking us in here?'

'Why, of course, Miss Amber. I'm a-fixin' to kick some chimera butt.'

I looked at him dubiously. He'd done okay with the chair but I wasn't so confident about his skills against the chimera. However, I had no time to waste and Frogmatch was still growing, so Benjamin was up.

I pulled out my potions and paintbrushes. As I touched the walls and the wards lit up, I stared aghast at the forbidden black runes. This wouldn't be a quick fix. I mentally rolled up my sleeves and got painting. I tried hard not to get distracted from the sounds behind me. There was a crash and another yowl.

Benjamin laughed. 'Why, take that you little kitty-cat!'

I tried to tune him out and focus on the runes. One misstep and I'd make the whole room explode. No pressure.

'Benji!' Benjamin said aloud. 'It's good to have you back, my friend. We're fighting a chimera! Would you like to take over? I feel this is more in your skillset than mine.'

'Of course,' Benji replied politely. 'We are immune to her fire so it's only her claws we really need to worry about!'

'Oh my, I wish I'd known that. That sure is handy,' Benjamin crowed.

'The witches tried to think of everything when they made us. I gather there was an incident once with a chimera getting into the Coven chambers. Since then, all golems have been immune to their fire.'

'All right,' Frogmatch said. 'Let me at her! It's my turn.'

There were more yowls then Frogmatch let out a filthy string of swear words that would have made a sailor wince. 'That hurt, you damned big pussycat!' he complained.

I gritted my teeth and focused; I had to trust the men to deal with the chimera and keep it away from me. I kept painting. When I was certain I'd deactivated everything, I pulled my magic through the wards and ripped them down. My shoulders slumped with relief when no explosions followed. 'Okay.' I turned around. 'We can go.'

I blinked at the sight before me. Naturally, it wasn't going to be as easy as just walking out.

Chapter 46

Benji had his stone arms around the lion's throat and was choking it out, Frogmatch was doing the same to the snake head, and both chimera heads were gasping and thrashing. The goat head was rearing side to side, trying to get Benji or Frogmatch with her deadly horns so she could free her other heads.

I picked up another of the rickety chairs and slammed it down on her goat head with as much force as I could muster. The goat head slumped down, and the lion and snake quickly followed suit as Frogmatch and Benji strangled them. The chimera slid to the ground, unconscious.

I blew out a breath. 'Okay, let's go. Grab her.' I pointed to the still unconscious Ria; 'We'll take her with us.' Benji obligingly swung the teen onto his shoulder.

We'd already spent far too long in this room. I prayed that Oscar and my mum had managed to find the harkan

– and that Mum hadn't done anything stupid with it, like try and destroy it without me.

We ran out of the doorway then skidded to a halt. If I'd thought about it before, I would have wondered how Ria had clearly known the winding corridors so well that she'd unerringly threaded her way through them. Staring at the corridors stretching out before us, I had absolutely no idea how to get back to the library.

The pendant! I gave a mental head thunk and clutched at it. *Sisters!* I entreated urgently. *A little help!*

We will always assist, Princess, Abigay's warm voice reassured me. *But you need to brace yourself for what is coming.*

What is *coming?*

You saw the Goddess's vision. You know what must be done. Her voice was gentle.

I shook my head stubbornly. Just because I had seen myself crying with a blade in my hand, and just because a seer had told me I would kill my mother, didn't mean it was going to happen. I didn't believe in destiny, dammit.

The pendant glowed with a white light and rose up around my neck, gently tugging me forward, guiding me to the harkan.

All around us were the sights and sounds of fighting. The evil witches and the griffins were battling fiercely. I saw Apollinaire fighting with three necromantic-seized vampyrs and conceded that he was definitely on our side. Anway, now I knew why my father had lied about it; he'd given us a scapegoat, so that Ria could remain undetected.

I gritted my teeth. That lying bastard! Some small, desperate, part of me had wanted to believe him, wanted to trust him. He was my father, after all. I shouldn't have had the memory clearing broken because it had made the distant past so fresh. It had skewed my perception of him.

I wondered if Jeb had done something to my reclaimed memories of my father. They were still so strong; they should have weathered and settled in my mind but they hadn't. They'd been so present that I hadn't been thinking clearly. Well, I was thinking clearly now.

This ended today. I was going to destroy that damned harkan if it was the last thing I did.

Chapter 47

The pendant led us to the mahogany doors. I paused before I went in to reach out and feel Bastion. He was focused and frustrated; without immunity to the chimera's fire on his side, she was far harder to defeat.

I bit my lip. Bastion would shout at me but...

'Frogmatch, go and help Bastion with the chimera.'

The imp looked at me. 'He won't be happy with that.'

'Maybe not, but he'll still be alive. How long can you stay super-sized?'

'Not much longer,' he admitted. 'Five minutes maybe, tops.'

'So don't waste them with me. Go!' He hesitated a beat before he obeyed me.

I turned to Benji. 'In my vision, you were rescuing the truth seeker because we need her for some reason. Rescue her and bring her to me.'

Benji frowned. 'I don't want to leave you, Am Bam.'

'I concur,' Benjamin said. 'It is not wise to leave you unescorted, Miss Amber.'

'Wise or not, there is a reason the Goddess showed me the vision. Pop Ria down and go!' They didn't argue again, just propped Ria against the wall, turned and sank into the bricks.

I blew out a deep breath. Bastion would be really mad at me when he realised I had once again shaken off my guards. If we lived past this, I'd make sure to say sorry in a way that ensured he forgave me. We still hadn't done that thing he'd suggested that one time – I could try that. Maybe he'd forgive me then.

I reached for the brass knob on the door, turned it and walked into the library.

My father, Oscar and Mum were sitting down around a fire, looking for all the world as if they were having a chat. Oscar's rage filled eyes gave the game away – that and the way they darted pointedly back to the door behind me. He couldn't move but he was trying to warn me as best he could. He wanted me to turn around and walk away. I gave him a wry smile. Not today, Dad.

I met my father's eyes. 'Your other daughter is unconscious. She's propped against the wall outside.'

His gaze turned furious, though not with me. 'She had *one* job to do,' he groused. 'One. Stay under the radar; remain hidden. How hard is that to do?'

'Apparently pretty hard when you're a headstrong teenager.' I looked at him accusingly. 'You've fucked her up.' I rarely swore, but sometimes an expletive was needed. This was one of those occasions.

'Language,' Mum objected, with a stern glance.

'She wanted to kill her own mother,' I explained to her. 'Then she wanted to kill me to take my place and bond with the harkan.'

Mum glowered. 'You're right. Shaun did fuck her up. See?' she said to him. 'You would have screwed up Amber too if I'd given you half a chance.'

'I *loved* you,' he growled at her. 'And you threw me away and blackmailed me!'

'Bullshit!' my mother cursed. 'You had a whole other family, Shaun. Louisa, remember her? And your damned kids, Rebecca and Edward?'

'And Meredith,' I interjected. 'He married her too. Shaun is big into polygamy.'

'Don't call me Shaun!' he spat. 'Call me Dad.'

'No,' I refused flatly. 'That's reserved for Oscar.'

'Oh!' Mum's eyes filled with tears as she turned her head to look lovingly at Oscar, 'I'm so pleased.'

Oscar smirked at Shaun. 'Both your women love me.' He was trying to goad him but into doing what, I wasn't sure.

I needed to get this back on track. 'Where's the harkan?' I demanded.

'Here,' Shaun said calmly. 'Come and see it.' He tapped the clear glass box next to him. Through the translucent panes I could see the dark red crystal, glowing, pulsing with light like a visible throbbing heartbeat. I didn't need to touch the jewel to feel its evil intent. The power of the damned thing pervaded the room.

'Don't touch it!' Mum barked at me.

What did she think I was, an acolyte? I took a small step forward to take a better look at the clear box. As I was still swimming in the magic of three witches, I could easily see the snare runes all around it. I sighed. 'Bring it to me here. I'm not stepping into any of your traps.'

'Worth a try,' my father said, grinning at me unrepentantly. Shaun stood, crossed the distance between us and handed me the harkan box. I felt the weight of its power instantly; the box was containing it to a degree but even holding the box made the power vibrate into my fingertips.

'Let me get Ria,' Shaun sighed. 'I don't want her getting hurt in the fighting.' He went to the door and stepped out of the room.

I took advantage of his absence to quickly consult with my sisters. I grabbed the pendant in my left hand. *How do I destroy it?* I asked them silently.

It is made with a life force forcibly taken. It is destroyed with a life force freely given. Abigay's voice was calm.

I clenched my jaw. On some level, I had known it would come to this. I let the pendant drop back to my chest and across the room I met my mother's all-too-knowing eyes.

'It was my mistake,' she said softly, as if there were only us in the room. 'You know the prophecy, Amber. "Her sacrifice made in love's pure light."'

I shook my head stubbornly. 'No.'

'Yes,' she insisted.

Before we could argue further, Shaun returned cradling Ria in his arms. When he laid her down on the sofa, she looked like she was sleeping. Her face wasn't lined with malice and hate, and she looked so young.

Shaun reached into his pocket and pulled out Fido, who was barely moving. He pulled a vial of the familiar potion I'd made out of his pocket, poured a little onto the coffee table and laid Fido next to it. The mouse opened his eyes and sniffed the air.

'Drink it,' my father ordered him.

I remembered suddenly that Fido had ridden into the safe room on Lucille's back. I'd thought it was because they were messing around, but now I saw that Fido could barely move. I realised that Lucille had carried him out of necessity. Dammit, if I'd realised Fido was sick sooner, Ria's betrayal might not have blindsided me the same way. I had missed too many clues and now here I was, stuck in the spider's web with one heck of a tarantula.

Luckily, I've never been afraid of spiders.

Chapter 48

'Thank you for the potion,' my father said.

'Did you use it to heal Cesca?' my mum asked, looking around for my father's dog familiar.

Sorrow crossed his face. 'Cesca is no longer with us,' he admitted. 'The problem with bonds is that you can't have two at once.'

'Shaun?' My mother's voice whipped out, full of dread. 'What did you do?'

'I found a dark spell that would let me bond with a magical creature, but it demanded a sacrifice.'

Mum looked at him with horror. 'You killed your own familiar?'

'She volunteered. She knew that it was best for us,' he said evenly.

'What did you bond with?' I asked, but I already knew the answer.

'The chimera, of course. Her name is Lycia. And she hasn't been afflicted with the sickness like Cesca was.'

Pain suddenly wracked me – not mine but Bastion's. His agony took my breath away and I dropped to my knees. 'Bastion!' I gasped.

'Yes, I'm sorry about that,' Shaun said, his voice genuinely full of regret. 'But if you're going to bond with the harkan, you can't have another bond interfering with it. I've told Lycia to make it quick.'

I glared at him. 'When you went to get Ria, you gave the chimera some more instructions?'

'Yes,' he admitted. 'My bond with Lycia isn't as close as the one I had with Cesca – Lycia needs verbal commands. She was toying with him before. Now she's trying to kill him.'

'Tell her not to and I'll willingly bond with your damned crystal,' I promised. I was lying, but I hoped he didn't know that.

'I told you,' he said, looking sympathetic, 'you can't have two bonds.'

So that was why he'd wanted Bastion here.

Shaun had already known that Bastion was my familiar; he'd watched Bastion sit on the runes of truth and lie to the council that *he* had killed Hilary and connected the dots faster than I had. From that moment, he'd known that Bastion had to die in order for me to bond with the harkan.

But it turned out my father didn't know everything there was to know about bonds. You *can* have more than one at once; I already had two. 'And that's where you're wrong,' I said quietly. Then I shouted, 'Now, Fehu!'

The raven plunged down from his hiding place at the top of the bookshelf, claws outstretched as he attacked Shaun.

Mum leapt up from her chair, her arm dripping with blood. She'd surreptitiously been using her own blood to paint *ezro* on the runes that were binding her and Oscar. Oscar reached into his pocket and pulled out a lighter, grew the flames and sent them careening towards my father.

As Shaun sent Fehu flying into a wall with a burst of black power, his eyes turned black and a vampyr phased out of the shadows to absorb the flames that were heading straight for him.

Mum ignored Shaun and ran towards me. She grabbed the athame at my ankle and held it level with her heart. 'No!' I screamed, batting her hand down just as she dragged the blade towards herself. Rather than striking her heart, the athame plunged into her stomach and she let out an agonised gasp.

'Rune ruin, Amber!' she bitched at me. 'Now you've just made my death slower.'

'I can heal you!' I said desperately as I pulled off my tote bag, tore it open and pulled out the healing potions.

'That's not the point, Am,' she said softly. 'To destroy the harkan we need a willing sacrifice. I'm willing, Amber.'

'Well, I'm not!' I snapped.

Across the room, my father and Oscar were fighting. My father glanced across and took in the tableau of my mother and me, and suddenly a wave of black magic rolled out from him. It destroyed my healing potions instantly. 'You bastard!' I screamed at him.

'It's okay,' Mum said weakly, grasping my right hand. It wasn't. It absolutely wasn't.

My mum was dying but I still had one last option to save her. The world could go to hell for all I cared.

I reached into the harkan's box and seized the malevolent jewel in my left hand.

Chapter 49

'No!' Mum shouted. 'Put it down! Don't you dare bond with that thing!'

The jewel was so happy to see me that it crooned at me. It had been made sentient by my mother and so it loved me in the same way that she did. I was the harkan's dearest daughter, and together we could destroy so many things. We could kill anything and anyone we wanted; we could coat the world in blood and rune anything. We could use the dead bodies we made to create so many potions. We could achieve greatness unlike anything anyone else had ever achieved. The few that survived would worship us – and then we could open the gateways to the other Realms and destroy those too. I had always wanted greatness.

'Amber, darling, come back to me. Look at me!'

It took a real effort to wrench my eyes from the beautiful maroon depths of the harkan, and in my mind it hissed with displeasure as I took my eyes off it.

'Listen to me, love,' mum pleaded. 'I *need* to die, Amber. I need to right this wrong! Lucille can't preserve me much longer and I won't go back to being what I was! I won't go back to not knowing you and Oscar. I am done. This is *my* move and it's my choice to play it.'

And this is mine, said Abigay in my mind. *Don't you dare let her die, Amber. Tell my bestie that I love her.*

Seemingly of its own volition, the pendant around my neck rose and blazed with a white light that was so bright it was painful to behold.

The harkan sensed the threat and sent a cloud of black magic bubbling outwards, but the blinding white light from the pendant pierced the thick black ochre that clung to the jewel. Then the glowing pentagram dropped and touched the harkan itself.

The jewel screamed into the depths of my mind.

Across the room, my father screamed too. He dropped to his knees. 'Lycia!' he cried.

I felt a surge of satisfaction from Bastion and then he was on the move, coming closer to me. He'd killed my father's familiar but he was in such pain. I struggled to compartmentalise his agony.

In my hands, the malevolent jewel pulsed once and struck my mother with a flash of red magic before crumbling to nothing. As it folded in on itself, a huge shockwave of power flew outwards and I doubled over as it hit me like a punch to the solar plexus.

When I regained my breath, I looked at Mum. She was slumped on the floor, laid low by the harkan's final malevolent action, the pulse of red power that had struck her.

'Mum!' I screamed. I reached desperately for her neck and gasped with relief when I felt a thready pulse. But it wouldn't last for long, not with blood still pouring from her stomach – and the Goddess alone only knew what the harkan had done to her with its last pulse of magic.

I couldn't comprehend it. I hadn't stabbed Mum, not like the seer had said or like the Goddess's vision had shown me, but she was still dying and I had no healing potions left, thanks to my father's vile actions.

The door flew open and Bastion ran in. He was in human form, he had no shirt on and his chest was covered in agonising burns. Benji chose the same moment to walk out of the wall clutching the pale truth seeker to his chest. I struggled to acknowledge any of them as I stared in horror at Mum's chest that was barely rising and falling.

Bastion knelt next to me.

'I didn't stab her,' I said inanely. 'The seer said I would stab a blade into her heart and the vision showed that too, but I didn't. She stabbed herself. I don't understand. She's *dying*, Bastion.' A sob slipped out, then I was crying and I couldn't stop. Tears ran down my face, for once allowed to fall freely.

'Save her!' Oscar yelled at me across the room. 'You have to save her, Amber!' His voice was desperate.

I looked over and saw that he had hogtied Shaun and was holding a blade at his throat. Shaun was immobile; all the fight had left him at the death of his second familiar.

Bastion pulled his phone out of his pocket. 'Glimmer,' he growled at me. He dialled Jinx's number. 'I need Glimmer,' he said urgently when Jinx answered the phone. 'Now! Send it to me!'

He didn't wait for an answer, just held out his hands and waited. Like the harkan had been, Jinx's blade was sentient; it could also transport itself through space by sheer willpower.

My brain started to fire. Glimmer? How would the dagger help our situation? Jinx's magical blade took the magical essence of one being and gave it to another. It could turn a Common human into a werewolf or give a fire elemental the power of a water elemental; all it needed was the blood of the creature we wanted to create.

Glimmer landed in Bastion's hands. He grinned triumphantly then grasped the magical blade by the hilt and used it to cut into his arm, gifting the blade *his* blood. His magic-rejuvenating-healing blood.

Griffin's blood. My brain caught up with Bastion's plan. Of course! I took the blade from Bastion and, with tears streaking down my face, I plunged the blade into my mother's heart. Not to kill her – as the seer had thought – but to save her.

I pulled the magical dagger out and stared at her anxiously. 'Wait,' Bastion cautioned. 'It takes a moment to work. Watch her wounds.'

I watched. When her skin started to knit together and heal rapidly, I knew that Glimmer had done its job. She had been turned into a griffin. But her pulse was still thready and weak. She needed more than the fast-healing of a shifter; she needed a miracle.

Luckily, I had one handy. I reached into my left pocket and pulled out a vial of final defence. I unstoppered the potion that would save a griffin even an inch from death and poured it down her throat. She swallowed.

Her wounds vanished in an instant. Her eyes snapped open. 'Amber? What did you do?'

'Thank God!' Oscar whispered.

I burst into happy tears and flung myself into her arms. 'Mum! You're okay!'

'The harkan?' she asked urgently.

'Destroyed,' I managed, trying to get control of myself. I wiped my tears from my face.

'How?' she asked, sitting up.

I bit my lip and reached for my pendant. It warmed under my fingers. *Abigay?* I called.

She is gone, Edith whispered, her voice thick with sorrow. *Her sacrifice will be remembered.*

My hand fell from my pendant. 'Abigay,' I said softly. 'She gave her soul to the harkan. She wanted to save you. She told me to tell you that she loved you.'

For the first time that I could recall, my mother cried.

Chapter 50

Ria and Shaun were propped on the couch with anti-magic cuffs around their wrists, hands in front of them. Ria glared malevolently at me but my father was staring off into the middle distance, his face blank.

'And the harkan is definitely destroyed?' Inspector Stacy Wise asked.

I nodded. 'It disintegrated. I expect the power wave was felt for miles.' I rubbed my sternum.

Bastion wrapped an arm around me. He was still shirtless. After mum had been healed, he'd finally turned his attention to himself. A shift wouldn't heal his chimera-induced burns but the final-defence potion would. The burns had covered more than a third of his body; as he'd slammed into shock, he'd pulled out his vial of final defence and downed it.

We'd both gasped in relief as his raw, blistered flesh healed. Focused on saving Mum, he had tried to contain the agony, but when that urgent task had been completed he couldn't avoid it. It had been enough to make me whimper with pain – and it was my agony rather than his own that impelled him to use the potion. It was a relief to both of us when he'd healed completely.

'Has he said anything?' Wise asked, gesturing at Shaun.

'He's in shock,' I confirmed quietly. 'The death of his familiar is a hard blow to bear – and this was his second familiar.'

'I thought a witch only ever had one.'

'We do,' I confirmed grimly. 'But like for every rule, there are exceptions.'

'Kill me.' My father spoke suddenly and looked at me. 'I'd rather die than be arrested.'

I glared. 'This isn't about what you want but what I have to live with. I'm not down with patricide.'

'Then have Bastion kill me,' he said impatiently. 'The Connection will put me in the darkest cell and keeping out the Red Guard will be impossible. They'll torture me, Amber.'

'As you have done to so many,' I pointed out sharply.

'Is this justice, then?' he asked bitterly.

'I don't know what it is, but you're my father and I'll see you locked up and I'll see that you're safe,' I promised. Probably somewhat rashly.

'You always did have an overdeveloped sense of right and wrong.' He looked resigned.

'The Red Guard can't get into where you're going,' Wise said grimly. 'No one can. You'll be going to our most secure facility.'

My father's lip curled back in a sneer. 'HMP Wakefield? Then no doubt I'll be dead in the week instead of a day.'

Wise snorted. 'You're not going to Monster Mansion. Where you're going makes the Alcatraz of the Rockies look like an amusement park. You're going to a black site that no one knows exists. Even the Red Guard.'

Ria looked wide-eyed. 'I didn't do anything wrong! I'm innocent. I got led astray by my father! Don't send me to a black site!'

Meredith was being consoled by Melrose. She let out a sob but she didn't take a step towards her daughter. She'd been heartbroken when I'd told her that Ria had confessed to planning to kill her. I could see that she was still hoping it was all a dreadful misunderstanding.

The rescued truth seeker was pale and washed out. 'I can help,' she offered softly. She'd introduced herself as

Annabelle Beaufort before Wise had arrived. To prove she really was a truth seeker I'd had her question Apollinaire, just to be absolutely certain that my father was blowing smoke about that young man's allegiances. When questioned, he had confirmed his loyalty was to Shirdal and to Bastion. He had no knowledge of the Domini and did not belong to the clandestine organisation. Not that I'd had much doubt remaining, still, better to be safe than sorry.

'Who are you?' Wise asked brusquely, eyeing the pale woman who looked like a stiff breeze would blow her over. Annabelle had been part of the security at the soul auction, and she still looked as sick and gaunt as she had then. Captivity didn't agree with her.

'She's a truth seeker,' I confirmed. 'But she's not going to be in the file officially,' I added firmly. Truth seekers are a valuable commodity and the nefarious – like my father – would use and abuse her without hesitation. I would ask Bastion to give her a new identity and a new start somewhere far away from here. If she wanted it. The Goddess had told me I could trust her for a reason. I suspected the truth seeker would have more involvement in my life than just today.

Wise blew out a breath. 'Of course she isn't,' she sighed. She nodded at Annabelle. 'Do your thing and get the kid to tell the truth. We need to know what we're dealing with.'

Unlike truth runes, a truth seeker can compel you to talk. Annabelle reached out and touched Ria's wrist. 'Get away from me!' Ria yelled, but Wise held her in place.

'Do you intend to commit murder and other heinous acts?' Annabelle asked.

'Of course I do! I plan to kill you all! I'll see you all dead and I'll dance on your fucking graves. I'll use the power from killing you to grow my powers as a necromancer until I get vampyrs to dance to my tune like my father did! I will raise the evil Coven above all and see you all rot like the weak pathetic beings you are! I will lie and manipulate my way to the top. I will use potions and poisons to help me succeed. I even gave Henry a potion to make him fall in love with me, so I could hear all about the coven's innerworkings from Ethan. Though he was annoyingly tight-lipped. I was going to drug him next. There is nothing I won't do to succeed.'

It was terrifying and sickening, hearing my own ambitions spouted back at me, but worse. Like me, she had been born with a need to prove herself. But unlike me, her needs were twisted and warped; she would do *anything* to succeed. We weren't the same, I reassured myself. There was nothing wrong with ambition, nothing wrong with a drive to succeed, as long as you didn't harm anyone else to get to the top. That was the difference between her and me.

'Can you ask her about her poisoning?' I asked tightly. 'She took a vial of black mordis once; I want to know her motivation for that. She couldn't have known that I'd be able to save her.' A vial of black mordis inevitably meant death. I'd worked for hours to create a whole new potion just to save her. The thought left the taste of ash in my mouth.

Annabelle repeated my question, using her magic to force Ria to answer.

Ria sniffed. 'It was a weak watered down vial of mordis. Barely a drop of real mordis in it. It would have put me into a coma and then Madame X was going to awaken me secretly – letting it seem like I'd had my very own miracle. Instead you put your oar in and rescued me before Madame X could.' She glared at me. 'You ruined everything. I was going to have such a dramatic reawakening. I would have been the centre of attention but instead everyone was talking about *you*. I was going to kill you for that alone.'

Meredith slumped back into Melrose's arms and covered her face with her hands. 'Goddess,' she moaned.

Ria snorted. 'Don't appeal to that weak-willed wench. She gives you barely half the power you should have. Better to devote yourself to Hel – she is a goddess worth worshipping! Let her dark power consume you and you will rise again, stronger than ever.' Ria started to laugh. She sounded distinctly unhinged. Hel was the Goddess of death. I shuddered, better to worship Satan than Hel.

Next to her, Shaun sighed. 'She never did learn the power of subtlety. Some people are unteachable.' Without blinking, he reached over to his daughter with his cuffed wrists, but it wasn't to comfort her. He grabbed her head and twisted, snapping her neck.

Ria dropped to the sofa, lifeless.

'She was a liability.' He shrugged nonchalantly.

My mouth dropped open. Part of me couldn't process what had just happened. I gaped at my father. For all my dad had made familial noises, just like that, he'd killed his daughter. A cold weight settled in my stomach. There would be no redemption for Ria now. Somehow, I'd still hoped that she might be rehabilitated. But now there would be nothing at all for Ria but the Goddess's judgement.

'Fuck,' Wise said and gritted her teeth. 'This is a cluster-fuck.' She stepped forward and reached out to touch Ria's broken neck, to verify death. After a moment, she pulled her fingers away and shook her head.

Meredith screamed.

Chapter 51

I flew on Bastion's back as he took us to the nearest city, Edinburgh. Oscar was driving my mum, Benji and Frogmatch back there, but I needed some time to process the gargantuan pile of poop that had just gone down.

Watching my father being taken away in cuffs – behind his back this time – was not a highlight in my life. And it wasn't over yet because my dear, murderous half-brother, Edward, was still on the loose somewhere.

Beatrice Wraithborne had been one of the evil witches who had fought to keep the house standing. As she'd sent dark magic careening towards Bastion, she had taunted him that her texting him my location was part of the Leader's plan all along, a plan to bring Bastion in so that he would die.

As Bastion was busy with Lycia, it was Frogmatch that had dealt with the evil witch. When he had shrunk down to his usual pint size, he had scuttled across the floor and tied her laces into an intricate work of art. When she had tried to curse him, his impish magic had awoken. The elaborately tied laces had grown and extended upwards, growing into dark and deadly vines. The insidious plant had crept up her body whilst she had attempted to summon dark magic to destroy it. The vines had moved faster and faster. They had wrapped around her slim neck and strangled her whilst she pawed at them in panic. Apparently, Frogmatch's knot designs weren't just about aesthetics.

Wise was going to send me a full list of the dead when they'd been identified. There was an horrific room of the dead in the evil Coven's basement: vampyrs in cages, dead bodies in various states of dismemberment, and what looked like a wall of trophies. It was in that room of horror that I had found small Fifi, Hannah's snake familiar. She had been nailed to the trophy wall. Bastion had removed the nail at my request. It had taken every inch of bravery that I possessed to pick up the serpent and take her back with me, albeit in a box. However terrified I was of reptiles, it was the right thing to do; I would fulfil my vow to see the small snake resting with her mistress.

As well as the corpses in the macabre room of the dead, Charlize and Haiku had been a little enthusiastic in some of their dispatches. Dental records would be needed to identify a good portion of the fresh bodies that lay strewn around the manor.

I had called Voltaire and told him about the vampyrs in the cages. Wise probably wouldn't like that move, but Voltaire *had* brought David to me and saved Benji's life. I figured with the phone call we were square.

We left when the mansion was overrun with Connection operatives; as more vans arrived, it was time to make a discreet exit. Bastion flew us over Edinburgh's castle, but he didn't bank to the Witchery as I'd expected; instead, he flew us over Dean Gardens before landing in front of an impressive Georgian house.

I slid off his back and he shifted to human. 'Erm, Bastion, where are we?'

He shrugged. 'One of my houses.'

'One of... How many houses do you have?'

'A few. Come on.' He unlocked the front door and tugged me inside. The house was warm and softly lit.

Apollinaire greeted us. 'Dinner is in the kitchen boss.' He gave us both a little bow and left through the front door, locking it behind him and leaving us alone.

'You sent Apollinaire ahead to get us dinner?' I asked incredulously.

'And to warm up the house. She's old and it takes a while.' He patted the walls affectionately. 'Let's eat first and then we'll talk.'

He tugged me along, letting me gape at the luxurious house. Most of the rooms had floor-to-ceiling bookcases. 'Ah, Bastion, what's with all the books?'

He sent me an amused book. 'You're not the only reader here, Bambi. My tastes lean more towards Clancy and Grisham rather than Nora Roberts, but I am a reader.'

'I think I love you even more,' I breathed, looking at the laden bookshelves.

He barked a laugh. 'Good to know.' My stomach rumbled. 'Come on, let's get the beast fed.' He led me to a modern kitchen with a large oak dining table. Apollinaire had gone all out and lit some candles for us at one end of the gargantuan table.

'This is huge!' I exclaimed.

'Said the actress to the bishop,' Bastion quipped, making me snort. 'I host a lot of griffins here sometimes. It's nice to have an informal entertaining space.'

He guided me to the table before opening a bottle of white wine. He poured us both a glass before getting two plates out of the oven. 'Careful,' he murmured as he set the food down. 'The plates are hot.'

Apollinaire had made – or sourced – deliciously cooked seabass in some sort of white wine and caper sauce resting on a bed of buttery new potatoes and crushed minted peas, decorated with samphire. I gave an appreciative moan. 'This is phenomenal.'

Bastion looked at me over the rim of his glass. 'You'll make that noise for me later.'

'Promises, promises,' I said a shade breathlessly.

He smiled. He knew he could deliver.

I smiled back. So did I.

Chapter 52

I woke aching in the best way as Bastion pressed a kiss to my shoulder. 'Morning, Bambi. How are you feeling today?'

I considered. 'I don't know. We dealt a significant blow to the evil Coven last night, not just in getting my father arrested. The griffins were pretty slasher-happy. There were lots of dead bodies on the floor. We've cut off the head of the snake.'

'With a poison like that, it's not enough,' Bastion noted. 'We need to root it all out.'

I sighed. 'I know. I've begun to realise why the position of Crone is one for life. I don't think I'll ever be done hunting evil witches. It's like the Forth Bridge: by the time you've finished painting it once, it's time to start painting it all over again.'

'I have faith in you,' he murmured, 'but you can't influence human nature. Some people just want power and they don't care how they come by it.'

Once I might have been counted amongst that number. I'd wanted to be the Symposium witch member; I'd wanted to be remembered with such zeal that I might even have crossed a line or two. Things had changed now, though. I didn't care anymore about being remembered; I cared about living my life in the *right* way, bringing about positive change for myself and those around me.

I still didn't want kids, which was good because the Crone position didn't allow for a family even though it allowed for a husband. Hmm, now there was a thought. 'Do you want to get married?' I asked Bastion as I trailed my fingers over his washboard abs.

He blinked. 'Are you proposing?'

'No, we're discussing. Hypothetically, one day, would you like to marry me?'

He pulled me into his arms and kissed me thoroughly. 'Today, tomorrow, any day,' he promised. 'I'm a fan of wedding cake. And wedding nights.'

'I'm serious,' I huffed.

'So am I.' He propped himself up on one arm. 'I love you, Amber DeLea. And I'm more than happy to spend the rest of my life showing that to you.'

He kissed me again and this time he accompanied it with a big ball of love that he threw down our bond to me. He loved me, he wanted to spend every waking moment with me, he wanted to grow old with me and he *definitely* wanted to marry me.

'Oh,' I said when we came up for air.

'Oh,' he repeated with a grin. 'For some reason, I find I can't be without my irascible sassy witch. And I don't want to be. I'm ready for forever whenever you are. Just say the word and I'll put a ring on it.'

I grinned. 'Not today. But soon.'

'I'll take soon.' And that was the last we said for a long while.

Chapter 53

The Coven Council was in a flap. Not that I could blame them: we had nine dead evil witches, according to Wise's list. With my father behind bars, that left at least five more in hiding in the Covens. The revelation of Beatrice's true allegiance had been an understandable shock.

I was incredibly pissed off to see Seren was still alive and well, though frankly she was too dumb to be an evil witch. She would have tipped off her Coven in the first week by stealing too many hydration potions. She was a bitch – but that didn't make her evil. More's the pity.

'We need to commence the application process for others to join the Coven Council,' I said firmly. 'With the deaths of Felix, Hilary, Tristan and Beatrice, we need to recruit urgently. We need a minimum of seven to convene the Council, and at the moment we only have nine. All we need is a bout of flu and we won't have a quorum. I suggest we invite Eleanora Moonspell to apply. Does anyone else have any likely candidates?'

I thought of Jeb's comments about the inequality between men and women. What I wanted to aim for was equality. 'We could do with some more men, if any can be encouraged to apply.'

'I know a few who may be interested,' Carl confirmed gruffly.

'As do I,' Isadora confirmed.

'Excellent. That's a good starting point, especially as the Symposium will be sitting from next week and Kass will need to be in Liverpool for that.' I cleared my throat. 'I also need to hand over my position of Coven Mother of the Hula Coven.' I spoke the nickname with affection.

'Who do you propose?' Rosalind asked.

'Ethan Hawksbane,' I offered.

'He's a man!' Seren objected, scandalised.

I offered her a flat look. 'Clearly. He is also the most qualified witch to take over running the Coven. It has come to my attention that some of the men feel somewhat hard done by. Save for a position on the Coven Council, there is not much opportunity for them to progress – and for some, the only option to attain further power is to join the evil Coven. I wish to remove that as a motivation. What we should be striving for is equality. So I suggest that we make Ethan our first Coven Father.'

Jasper pounded on the table. 'Hear, hear!' he said pompously.

Arthur's fist slammed on the table. 'Aye.' Satisfaction glimmered in his eyes.

Carl nodded and tapped two fingers on the surface of the table. 'Aye.'

All three men looked at the women.

Isadora let out a huff. 'Well obviously I'm all for equality.' She tapped the table twice. 'Aye.'

Seren folded her arms. 'Absolutely not. Nay.' The others ignored her like she hadn't spoken.

'Aye,' said Kass firmly, rapping the table with her knuckles.

Octavia and Rosalind both hit the table at the same time. 'Aye.'

I relaxed. 'The Ayes have it. With the Coven Council's permission, I will travel to my former Coven to deliver the news in person – and pack my things up, of course.'

'You'll be moving to the Witchery?' Octavia asked.

'No. I have another home, on Ann Street.'

'On Ann Street?' Jaspar let out a low whistle. 'Well now, you're doing well for yourself, lass.'

I smiled but said nothing more on the subject. 'One final piece of business. The golem known as Benjamin has unfortunately been compromised. Due to a deactivation, his crystal heart is no longer guiding his actions and he can no longer be compelled by the council. I propose that we remove him from Coven Council duties.'

Octavia frowned. 'We can't just let a golem loose on the streets of Edinburgh,' she groused.

'I will take full responsibility for his actions,' I soothed. 'He will reside with me on Ann Street.'

Kass shrugged. 'If you're happy to take responsibility for him, that's one less issue for the Council. Personally, I don't condone the process of permanent deactivation for the golems once their use is done, so that's a handy solution. We have David, and another golem is being created as we speak, ready for awakening should the need arise. Any objections?' She looked around the depleted circle and moved on rapidly. 'None heard,' she said briskly. 'The golem known as Benjamin passes to the Crone.' She rapped her knuckles down.

I grimaced internally; I hated that Benji was being passed to me like chattel – but one thing at a time. 'Thank you. I leave you to make the announcements of the dead and to begin the application process so that the Council can once again enjoy full strength. I strongly suggest that all applicants are questioned upon truth runes.'

'There will be outrage!' Octavia gasped.

'Better there be outrage than more evil witches on this damned Council,' Carl growled.

'Aye,' Jaspar agreed fervently.

'Aye,' said Isadora.

'Oh fine, aye,' huffed Seren.

'Excellent.' Business concluded, I stood to leave. I gave Kass's shoulder a quick squeeze and mouthed at her "Drinks soon?" She grinned and nodded. I turned to the assembled Coven Council, such as it was, and offered a small bow. 'Goddess guide you all.'

Then I swept out with Bastion on my heels.

Chapter 54

My mum was talking to David at the door to the Coven Council, with Oscar hovering protectively around her. She smiled when she saw me. 'Amber!' As was my habit now, I searched her eyes. They were clear and fixed on *me*; since the destruction of the harkan, she hadn't once slipped back to her dementia-ridden days.

Lucille chittered a greeting at me as she gambolled around Mum's feet. I knelt down and stroked her, happy to see her energy was back after she had been so close to death's door. She really had given virtually everything to keep Mum present, and it had nearly cost her life.

'How are you?' I asked anxiously. Mum had been checked over by a number of healers, me included, but no one had found any lingering ill-effects from the blast of red magic the harkan had shot at her.

'I'm okay,' she said easily. 'Charlize has been teaching me about partial shifting today.'

'Any signs of any ... urges?'

Mum shook her head. 'None.'

She had quickly acclimatised to the idea of being a griffin, especially when it transpired that she still had all of her witch magic. She could still rune with the best of them. So far, the griffins' urge to kill didn't seem to have been passed on to her. Glimmer's gifts are always a little odd. When Jinx's friend Hester was turned into a vampyr using Glimmer, she didn't have any urge to drink blood; similarly, Mum seemed to have no griffinish urge to kill.

'That's good.' I waited a beat before asking, 'And what exactly are you doing here?'

'Trying to eavesdrop,' she replied guilelessly. 'But David here wouldn't let me get close enough to paint any runes.'

'I should hope not,' I said, amused. 'Why are you trying to eavesdrop?'

'I'm bored,' she admitted. 'It was actually easier when I only had half my faculties and I was happy painting all day. Now I'm all me, I don't have the attention span for oil paintings. I have no coven to run, and nothing to do.'

I grinned. 'I have it on good authority that some positions on the Council are coming up.'

Mum brightened. 'Now there's an idea!' She turned to Oscar. 'What do you think Oz?'

Oscar smiled. 'You can do anything you put your mind to.'

She grinned. 'Damn right I can.' She linked her arm through his. 'I want to put my mind to...' She lowered her head to whisper to Oscar.

Next to me, Bastion reddened. I raised an eyebrow questioningly. 'No,' he murmured. 'Trust me, you don't want to know. I'll try and expunge the images she just conjured into my mind. I did *not* need to know that about my future in-laws.'

I felt my own face redden as my seventy-year-old mum giggled coquettishly. 'Maybe we could get our minds cleared,' I suggested.

'You always have the best ideas.' Bastion grinned. 'Now come on, we only have an hour before the meet with Voltaire.'

Chapter 55

We met Voltaire in Greenwoods café; he was already sitting at a table when we entered. I ordered a cappuccino and a blueberry muffin before joining him. To my surprise, he stood as I approached and gave *both* Bastion and I a respectful bow. 'Crone,' he greeted me. 'Bastion.'

'Voltaire.' I kept my voice level, like his greeting hadn't wrongfooted me. Whoever had heard of a Red Guard being friendly with a witch? I remembered his comment about Abigay; maybe it wasn't me he respected but my mantle. My whole job now was to weed out evil witches and his role was much the same. I supposed that once again our interests were aligning.

I surreptitiously painted a couple of runes onto the table to prevent our conversation from being overheard.

'Thank you for meeting with me,' he started, when the runes were complete. All this respect coming out of his mouth felt plain wrong, like any second he was going to pull out a camera and reveal it was all a big prank. I resisted the urge to look around for cameras.

'Of course,' I said brusquely. 'What can I assist you with?'

'I am grateful for the phone call that alerted us to the events that transpired at the manor. I understand a significant blow has been dealt to the evil Coven.'

I nodded, keeping my face blank. 'Indeed.' If he was here to ferret out further information from me, that made a little more sense. He needed to play nice.

'I also understand that a necromancer was recently discovered within your own Coven.'

That was technically incorrect because there were actually two necromancers: Jeb and my father. Ria had been an apprentice of sorts. She hadn't yet attained the skills to call herself a necromancer, though her confessions under Annabelle's guidance had shown she was well on her way to doing so.

'Indeed.'

'And that they were dealt with appropriately?'

'I killed him,' Bastion said with a shrug.

Voltaire beamed. 'Wonderful.'

'I'm glad you called me here because another issue needs to be discussed,' I started.

'Of course,' he said expansively. 'Go on.'

'You must have a significant number of vampyrs missing because they keep attacking me.' I didn't censor my annoyance.

Voltaire grimaced. 'We do not have vampyrs missing *officially*. As such, we're conducting internal investigations. The obvious conclusion is that someone is turning vampyrs on an unauthorised basis.'

'The Connection is going to lambast you,' I noted.

'The Connection isn't going to find out, is it?' For the first time in our little tête-à-tête his voice was hard.

'What about the vampyrs at the evil witches mansion?' I asked.

'Unregistered with any clans.' He kept his face blank. 'They also disappeared from their cells before they could be taken into Connection custody.'

'You phased them out?'

'Of course not,' he said lightly. 'I had nothing to do with their extraction.'

Uh-huh, sure. I rubbed my face. However Voltaire had gotten the vampyrs out, it didn't really matter. I wasn't a tattletale and, frankly, I didn't want the Connection in my business any more than he did. 'The Connection won't hear about the rogue vampyrs from me,' I said.

Voltaire relaxed and smiled again. 'Good. Do you have any more information or leads you wish to share with us at this time?'

I wasn't one to look a gift horse in the fangs. 'We believe there are still five evil witches operating within the UK,' I told him.

He leaned forward, eyes gleaming. 'Any leads on their identities?'

'None of the dead from the recent skirmish were rune masters,' I admitted. 'And I witnessed a black witch killing someone remotely using complex rune spreads. They could have studied in secret—'

'But it's likely one of your rune masters is an evil witch.' He paused. 'Nice re-brand by the way. Entirely appropriate.'

'I thought so. And yes, it is likely that one of the rune masters is one of the evil witches.'

'Excellent. We'll get right on that.'

'Excellent,' I echoed. 'And Voltaire?'

'Yes?'

'I have started our new working relationship in the spirit of co-operation. If you do not share information in the same vein, a conversation like this will never happen again.'

He met my eyes before giving another bow. 'Understood, Crone. I will be in touch.' He walked away, leaving me to finally eat my blueberry muffin in peace.

Bastion watched him leave. 'You don't trust him, do you?'

I smiled faintly as I sipped my cappuccino. 'Not in the slightest. Can your hacker friend Incognito get a tap on Voltaire's phone?'

Bastion grinned. 'That right there is why I love you.'

'Because I'm cynical?'

'Because you're sneaky. People love to underestimate you and it has become one of my greatest joys in life to watch you sucker punch them when they don't expect it.'

I smiled. 'You say the nicest things.'

Bastion pulled out his phone and tapped a message. 'Inc's on it.'

Perfect.

Chapter 56

I looked dubiously at Benji. 'What do you mean, you can drive?'

'Oscar has been showing me,' Benji said. 'Now that Oscar is guarding Luna full time, you need a new driver.' He puffed out his chest. 'I'm an excellent driver.'

'Do you have a licence?' I asked, not quite sure which answer I was hoping for. I *did* need a new driver, after all.

'Well ... no,' Benji confessed. 'Not exactly.'

I bit the inside of my cheek to stop myself from smiling. 'You'd better get that before you become my official driver,' I said evenly. 'The police get grumpy when you drive without a licence.'

Benji sighed. 'I suppose.'

'Soon,' I patted his cold arm. 'I bet you'll pass the test really quickly, and then you can drive me everywhere.'

He brightened. 'I will pass the exams really fast. I've been studying the theory. I know all the signs, like that one there for diverted traffic!' He frowned. 'Why are there two diverted traffic signs pointing in the opposite direction? The book did not cover this scenario.'

I looked to where he was pointing and let out a sigh. 'Frogmatch!' I huffed. 'Change it back!'

Snickering, the little red imp grabbed the second sign and moved it back down the road, making sure it pointed the correct way this time.

Bastion slid into the passenger seat, and Benji and Frogmatch joined him in the back.

'Let's get this show on the road,' Benjamin drawled. In an aside to Frogmatch he added, 'I've always wanted to say that.'

I ignored the chatter in the car and moved off, pointing us towards the Home Counties and what would be *my* Coven for only the next few hours.

It was raining when we pulled up, which matched my suddenly sour mood. It truly was the end of an era. Feeling somewhat melancholy, I parked in the underground carpark, touched the walls and lit up the familiar wards. This Coven tower had been my home for so long; though I was looking forward to the next chapter in my life, the next time I came here it would be as a visitor.

I turned, only to be engulfed in Bastion's arms. He kissed the top of my head but said nothing. He knew how I was feeling, and he offered silent, non-judgemental, comfort. He always knew the best thing to do to soothe me.

'Benji, Frogmatch, could you two go up and start packing up my bathroom and kitchen items for me?' I asked, more to get them out of the way than anything, though it did need doing.

'Sure thing,' Frogmatch threw me a cheeky salute.

'Of course,' Benji confirmed, proud at being given a trusted job. 'I'll bubble wrap your mugs,' he promised.

The two of them headed on up. I threaded my fingers through Bastion's and climbed the Coven stairs to where Ethan and Jacob lived. It was early evening, so the family were eating dinner together when I knocked. 'Sorry to intrude,' I apologised. 'Can I come in?'

'Of course, Coven Mother.' Jacob gave me a bow and stepped back.

Henry was slouched at the table, looking glum. 'Everything okay, Henry?' I asked.

He sighed. 'Sarah dumped me.'

'I'm sorry to hear that.'

'She feels bad about betraying Ria, but Ria hasn't been in touch with either of us in weeks,' he huffed.

I sat down. 'About that...' I explained the truth about Ria and Shaun as calmly as I could. Ethan and Jacob held hands as I listed some of the horrors Ria had confessed to. 'She also admitted that she had drugged you, Henry. An infatuation potion. That's why you felt so desperate to be with her for a while, and then it just ... stopped. It wasn't you not missing her anymore, it was the potion getting out of your system.'

Henry gaped for a moment then brightened. 'This is great! Sarah will be sure to give me another chance now.' He pushed back from the table. 'Can I go and see her?' he asked his fathers.

They deferred to me. 'Can Ria's betrayals be public knowledge?' Jacob asked.

I nodded. 'I don't intend to bury it.' Instead, I'd use her as the poster girl of what would happen to you if you turned to pain and torture to fuel your magic. Power really wasn't everything. But the worst of the news was still to come. 'But there's more. I'm sorry to say that when Ria started talking, the leader of the evil Coven killed her.'

Henry stilled. 'Ria's dead?'

I nodded. 'I'm sorry.'

Henry's eyes filled and painful silence stretched. Jacob and Ethan both reached out to touch their son. Henry's lip trembled. His jaw clenched and he dashed angrily at the tears that fell from his eyes. 'I know she drugged me and did bad things but we grew up together. She was my first—' he looked at his parents '—kiss,' he ended lamely.

'I know. I'm sorry,' I repeated.

'Why? You didn't kill her.'

'No,' I agreed, 'I didn't. But I'm sorry for your loss all the same.' I'd told them the truth about Shaun in that I'd said he was the leader of the evil Coven, but I hadn't said that he was my father. That felt private and it wasn't something I wanted to spread around. My business was my own.

Henry scrubbed at his eyes again. 'It's okay to cry,' I said suddenly. 'No one will think any less of you.'

He gave me a wobbly smile. 'I think I'm in shock. I don't know what to feel. I need to talk it over with someone. Can I go and see Sarah? Can I tell her about all of this?'

I nodded. 'Do what you need to do to process it.' I looked at his fathers. 'If it's okay with your parents, of course,' I added hastily.

'It's fine,' Jacob said softly. 'But come home tonight. We'll talk more this evening, as a family.'

Henry excused himself and gave his parents a quick hug. When he had left to spread the bad news, I turned to Ethan. 'Obviously, as Crone I can no longer maintain the position of Coven Mother.'

He nodded tightly, but I could see tension in the lines of his mouth. Not so long ago, I would have been thinking of Meredith or Hannah to replace me, but Hannah was dead and Meredith would be grieving the loss of her daughter for some time. The last thing she needed was a Coven to run. And besides, some of Jeb's griping had struck a chord with me. Bar his gender, Ethan *was* the right person for the role; he'd been doing it for weeks.

I cleared my throat. 'I would like to ask you to become the first Coven Father.'

Ethan froze then his eyes welled with tears. Jacob let out a sob and barrelled into his husband's arms.

'I—' Ethan started. He shook his head and buried it in Jacob's shoulder for a moment. Finally he took a steadying breath. 'It would be an honour,' he said. 'Thank you, Coven Mother. What about the application process?'

I shook my head. 'Your appointment has been ratified by the Coven Council. If you want the job it's yours, no application process needed. Frankly, you deserve it. I can think of no one else who would better lead our Coven. *Your* Coven,' I corrected myself, giving his arm a squeeze. 'I'm packing up my flat now and I'll be out of your hair as soon as I can.'

Ethan smiled at me. 'Thank you for this opportunity, Crone. I promise I won't squander it.'

'Of that,' I smiled back, 'I have no doubt.'

We had a small party in the Coven common room. I let Ethan handle the announcements – better to start as we meant to go on. After a brief show of my face, I excused myself to carry on packing.

Even with Benji, Bastion and Frogmatch helping, it took longer than I'd expected to pack up my whole life. Nevertheless, in a few hours, we were back on the road again. Despite the late hour, we decided to drive back to Edinburgh, mostly because I didn't want to step on Ethan's toes but also because I wanted to start living my life with Bastion.

Edinburgh, that siren of cities, was calling me home.

Chapter 57

We had returned home in darkness and tumbled into exhausted sleep. Benji and Frogmatch were ensconced in a guest room each. Bastion's home had five bedrooms so there was more than enough space for us all. Which was good, because I'd promised Benji would live with me. Luckily Bastion had been more than happy with that arrangement, for now at least.

When I woke, Bastion was already up and exercising. He'd had his home privately warded by Kass, and on top of that it had a state-of-the-art security system which was being monitored by one of the griffin security companies that Shirdal ran. All that security meant that Bastion could relax here in a way that I hadn't seen before. He was actually willing to leave my side, which was nice, but I also found I missed his steadying presence.

I showered, runed and dressed for the day. I sat in front of the mirror to say my affirmations, but found that today I didn't need to say them. I *did* have a familiar, and I was a strong and successful witch. I did need someone though – more than one someone. I needed Bastion, I needed Oscar and my Mum, and I needed Benji and Frogmatch. And none of that needing made me any the weaker – if anything it made me stronger. What a shame it had taken me forty-two years to realise that friends and family are a strength in life, not a weakness.

I squared my shoulders and re-framed the thought. I was grateful that I'd discovered friends and family were a strength.

Anyway, I had a new affirmation. 'I am a strong, successful witch. With my friends and family beside me, I am unstoppable. I *will* change this world for the better.' I smiled. It was true, and I was working towards it every day. I was going to build this Coven Council up into something I was proud to be a part of, and then I was going to go evil-witch hunting. Between me and Voltaire, we'd weed out those last five. And I'd make damned sure no one else thought that joining the evil Coven was a good idea.

I made my way down to the kitchen where I stopped abruptly. One wall of the kitchen had been made into a huge mug shelf. It hadn't been there when we'd left for the Home Counties Coven yesterday, but here it was. Neatly painted, it was a whole wall of little individual cubbies for each of my mugs, and Bastion had already unpacked them and set them in their new homes. I gaped at it. It was like a bookshelf, but for mugs.

'Do you like it?' Bastion murmured from behind me.

I whirled round and flung myself at him. 'I love it. Thank you so much!'

He smiled. 'I want this to be as much your home as mine. If you want to change anything, different décor or furniture, you just have to say.'

I shook my head. 'Your home is beautiful Bastion. Maybe with time I'll want to add little things here or there, but it really is lovely just as it is.'

'I'm glad. This house is special.' He reached out and patted the walls again. This time, I could have sworn there was almost a shiver running through the house. Bastion hesitated a second, looking at me. 'Are you hungry?'

My tummy growled, making him laugh. 'I could eat.' I shrugged nonchalantly. He pressed a kiss to my hair and released me. He strode to the fridge and pulled out a bowl of overnight oats and a glass of freshly squeezed orange juice. My eyes filled with tears at the thoughtful gesture. 'Thank you,' I managed.

He frowned. 'I broke the juicer,' he confessed. 'I'll have to ask Oscar which brand he used. Or maybe I just did it wrong.'

I smiled. 'I didn't think you knew how to do things wrong.'

'It's rare, but it does happen,' he admitted. He looked serious. 'I'm not perfect, Amber. I try to be – for you – but I'm not.'

'I know who you are, Bastion. I know every inch of your heart.'

He smiled. 'I have something to show you. I thought it could wait, but it turns out it can't.'

'What about my oats?' I protested half-heartedly.

'Fuck your oats.'

'That wouldn't be sanitary.'

He snorted a laugh. 'Come on witch. I want to amaze you.'

'You already do,' I admitted.

He tugged me out of the kitchen towards what I'd thought was a walk-in larder; instead it had a trapdoor under it. He pulled it up, locked it open and led me down some stairs. 'If this is where you kill me,' I quipped as I followed him into the darkness, 'I'll die happy.'

As we came to the bottom of the staircase, Bastion flicked on a light and my jaw dropped.

We were in a state-of-the-art potions laboratory. It made my secret laboratory back at the Coven tower look like a supplies cupboard. He had thought of everything. There were stainless-steel worktops and wooden work-tops and marble worktops. There were cauldrons of every shape, metal and size. There were tripods and lids and a rack full of paintbrushes.

Bastion tugged me forwards to a metal door. He pulled it open to reveal a walk-in fridge full of potions. They had neat little 'use by' dates marked on them.

'Brewed by Eleanora Moonspell,' he confirmed. 'I thought that you could set up your own free clinic here, once you get the Coven Council to allow you to give free medical aid legally, of course.'

I was speechless, possibly for the first time in my life. I gaped at him, my mind frozen in wonder at all that he had done for me. I would *love* to start my clinic again; free access to healthcare was something I was completely passionate about.

'One last thing,' he said, as he pulled me forward. 'I have another book for you.' He reached behind himself to a bookshelf and pulled out a book. This one was entitled *The Witch and the Griffin.* Half in a daze I took it, still somewhat in shock. I flicked it open and frowned when I saw that the pages were blank. 'It's empty,' I said in confusion.

I looked up from the book to see that Bastion was down on one knee before me. He was holding out a ring. 'Bambi, you said not today, but soon. Well, now is soon. I'm not always the best with words, but I love you. I love you with everything that I am and will ever be. I want a future with you. I want to write our own story into these pages. Amber DeLea, will you do me the honour of marrying me?'

I burst into inelegant sobs as I tried to nod, then I pulled him up so that I could bury myself in his arms.

'Is that a yes?' his low voice teased.

'Yes!' I burst out.

'Thank God,' he muttered, sliding the ring onto my finger.

I pulled back to try and examine it, but my eyes were so blurry it took a few attempts. Bastion hadn't given me a diamond ring; no – he knew me too well for that. Instead, he had given me a ring made of swirling runes: *algiz,* for protection; *fehu*, for love and luck – and for a joint familiar; *uruz,* for strength, and finally the lemniscate, the symbol for infinity.

A happy sob tore from my throat – it was perfect. I pulled him down to my lips, desperate to show him how I felt even though words escaped me. I kissed him with all of the passion in my heart and through our bond I *knew* that he accepted how much I loved him.

He was everything to me, and I would spend the rest of my life making sure that he knew it.

Chapter 58

After we had christened my new lab, we made our way back upstairs to finish the slightly warm overnight oats. I found myself staring at my left hand with a dopey smile on my face. I had given up on the dream of marriage a long time ago. With Jake in hiding, we could never have married openly.

I still missed Jake but I remembered him with fondness now. Jake was a part of my past that would never be unwritten; Bastion was a part of my future.

He nudged me. 'Hey,' he said softly, 'you okay? You're sad.'

I smiled. 'Only a little. Just thinking about Jake. We would never have been happy, not like you and I can be.'

'He loved you,' Bastion offered.

'I know, but not the way you do.'

'No,' he agreed, pulling me into his arms. 'No one will love you the way I do.' His fierce love rolled over me, scorching in its intensity. Luckily, I've always been a woman that likes heat.

Bastion pressed a kiss to my forehead. 'So, I've arranged for some of our friends to come for lunch.'

I blinked. 'We have friends?'

He grinned. 'As unbelievable as it is, yes, we do. I'd like to announce our engagement.' He paused. 'Only a few people know that I am your familiar. I am honoured and proud to be, but I think the depth of our bond is best kept between us. If enemies of mine learned that they could harm me through you...' He trailed off.

'You want to keep it secret that you are my familiar?'

'Secret make it seems sordid and it's not. But yes, I want to keep it need-to-know. Oscar and Luna know, obviously, and I have no issues with other friends knowing, but not the world at large. Is that okay with you? I know not having a familiar has been a big issue for you personally and professionally. If you would like to announce our bond—'

'No,' I interrupted firmly. 'I have no need to prove myself to anyone. Certainly not at the expense of either your safety or mine.'

'Are you sure? I don't want you to feel pressured.'

I laughed. 'Bastion, I agree with you. Stop trying to make an issue where there is none.'

The doorbell rang, saving us from further argument. By tacit agreement, we both went to get the door. To my surprise, there was a crowd on the doorstep. There was Oscar, Benji and my mum, as well as Shirdal and Charlize.

The latter's eyes instantly zeroed in on my ring, making it clear that she had been fully in the know about her father's plans. Charlize beamed at her dad and surreptitiously gave him a thumbs up, but she didn't say anything aloud. She was waiting for us to make the announcement.

'Come on in,' Bastion greeted them. Charlize gave him an extra big hug, and I smiled fondly as he kissed her hair. Next she barrelled into me. 'Congratulations!' she breathed so softly that I barely heard her. I gave her a big squeeze back.

'Your home is lovely, Bastion.' Mum smiled warmly at him. I met her eyes, still searching for *her* as had become habit, but she met my eyes with her own and smiled. 'Hello, darling.' She pulled me into a hug. 'I've put in my application to be part of the Coven Council. Fingers crossed for me. I'd forgotten how much I love Edinburgh. I find I'm quite ready for a change of scene.'

'Fingers crossed!' I replied lightly, feeling an unbelievable happiness burning in my chest. Even a matter of days ago, I wouldn't have believed that Mum and I could have a conversation, let alone that she might one day be able to resume a position in witching society.

I released her and hugged Oscar. I had missed him so much that tears stung my eyes. He embraced me just as hard and kissed my forehead. 'Hey kiddo,' he murmured, just for me.

'Hi, Dad,' I responded. 'I've missed you.'

'Back at you. The new norm will take some getting used to.'

'Yeah. Bastion made me some fresh orange juice.'

'He's a good man,' Oscar replied, his voice warm with approval.

'He is.'

Oscar and I hugged a moment longer; I wasn't ready to let go, and he made no movement to end the hug either. 'All right, Am?' he asked as I finally stepped back.

I smiled. 'Yes. I really am.'

Chapter 59

Bastion and I settled our guests. He took obvious delight in picking individual mugs for each one, trying to get a grin with his selection.

Benji gasped when he saw the wall of mugs in the kitchen. 'Now that is a work of art,' he grinned. 'I need to expand my own mug collection before I can rival that. Maybe I can put a shelf in my room.'

'Whatever you want to do,' Bastion said easily. 'The room is yours.' In reality, he hadn't just given Benji a room but a whole floor, including a bedroom and bathroom, a guest room and a reception room all of his own. The kitchen and dining room would have to be shared, but apart from that we had plenty of space from each other – not that I thought we'd need it.

'You've only just started your collection,' Bastion continued. 'I'm sure you'll have an extensive array of mugs before you know it. Birthdays and Christmases will soon build it up.'

Benji shrugged. 'I'm not sure exactly when my birthday is. July sometime.'

Anger flared. The Council hadn't cared enough to tell Benji when he had been made. 'I'll find out,' I promised. 'And then we'll hold a huge birthday party to make up for all the ones that we've missed.'

Shirdal raised his mug in salute. 'We'll make it the best damned party in the last century!'

Benji smiled wistfully. 'I'd like that.'

Benji grinned as Benjamin spoke. 'Why I declare, I would also love to experience a birthday party!' At the familiar sound of Grimmy's voice, Mum's head whipped around, searching for the grimoire.

'Ah, Benjamin? Why don't you go ahead and introduce yourself to my mother?' I suggested.

'I'm sure she'll recognise me, no matter my current physicality. Isn't that right, Miss Luna?'

She gaped. 'Grimmy? What happened? What the heck did I miss?'

'A lot, but this one is easily explained. Grimmy saved Benji's life, and there are two of them living in the golem now,' I explained briefly.

Mum slid a suspicious glance at him. 'I've never known you to be altruistic.'

'And I'm still not, Miss Luna,' Benjamin admitted. 'Whilst I reside in our dear friend Benji here, I get to *see,* to *feel,* to *touch.* It's fair to say I gained quite a lot out of saving Benji's life.'

Benji snorted. 'You did it because you liked me.'

'I do like you, young sir, that's the truth of it. And I'm heartily glad that we met when we did and the *manner* in which we did. You did Amber a great service by hiding me and keeping me safe. Now it is my honour to do the same for you.'

'Well,' Mum said. 'Well now. Isn't that something?'

The doorbell chimed again and my eyebrows shot up. 'More guests?'

Bastion smirked. 'I said I'd invited our friends.'

'Yes, but isn't this them?' I asked in genuine surprise.

He laughed. 'Come and see.'

We went to the front door together. I opened it to see a very tanned looking Jinx and Emory, with Reynard in tow. Reynard was shirtless as always these days, his black-feathered wings held neatly behind him like an avenging angel. 'Is the fucking love of my life here?' he asked eagerly.

'Shirdal?' I clarified.

'The one and only.'

'Yep, he's here.'

Reynard beamed.

'You look like you had an amazing honeymoon!' I said to the tanned couple. They exchanged a rueful glance. 'It was certainly something,' Emory muttered.

Jinx laughed and elbowed him in the ribs. 'No honeymoon talk today. We are here to celebrate Amber and Bastion.'

'What exactly are we celebrating about them?' Emory asked, just as Jinx saw the ring on my finger and gave a shriek of excitement. She bundled into me. 'Amber! Congratulations!'

I hugged her back stiffly, still unused to such affectionate exuberance, though I was certainly getting there. 'Thank you.'

She released me but she was still beaming. Emory's eyes zeroed in on my fingers and he grinned. 'Well, well! Bastion you old dog.' He clapped him on the shoulder, 'Congratulations!'

'You'll have to tell us all about the proposal,' Jinx said eagerly.

I looked at Bastion. 'It was perfect.'

'Awww,' Jinx smiled. 'You go all mushy when you look at him!'

I straightened. 'I do not!'

'Don't tell her,' Bastion murmured to Jinx as he gave her a welcoming kiss on the cheek. I felt a swell of familial affection from him towards her; he loved her like a niece.

I was going to suggest going inside the house when a movement down the garden caught my eye. Walking down the garden path towards us was Kass. '*Now* everyone has arrived,' Bastion said with satisfaction. 'Lucy and Manners can't make it but they send their love.'

I grimaced; I should really have touched base with Lucy now that I wasn't battling with evil witches and worried about the harkan. Although I guessed battling with evil witches was always going to be an ongoing thing.

Kass smiled. 'Hello. Am I the last to arrive?'

'But no less welcome,' I hastened to assure her. 'Come in, all of you.' I stepped back inside the house.

As Emory came in, he gave a low bow to me. 'Crone,' he greeted me formally.

'Prime Elite,' I responded in kind, with my own bow of respect.

Jinx mock glared at us. 'I sense politics. Bastion was very clear that no politics are allowed!'

I huffed a little. 'Well, what shall we discuss? Pop music?'

Jinx snickered at my open horror. 'Something like that. Or maybe wedding plans?'

'No one else has noticed the ring yet,' I noted. 'Not everyone is an observant PI.'

Emory sent me a wink. 'Amber, you look beautiful. Happiness suits you.'

I smiled at him. 'As it does you, Emory, as it does you.'

Kass tugged on my hand and I let her pull me back as the others preceded us into the kitchen. 'What's up?' I asked. 'Are you feeling okay?' I checked her over hastily. She looked good, with no sign of the heavy bags which sometimes plagued her eyes.

'I'm fine,' she assured me. 'I just wanted to talk to you privately for a moment. I assume your Mum's in there?' I nodded. 'Well, she's applied for a position on the Coven Council. We wanted to check how you feel about it before we do anything with her application.'

'We?'

'The Coven Council. We can bury her application if you think it will be awkward to work with your mum.'

I considered it for all of a heartbeat. Would it be awkward? At times, no doubt. Would she be an exemplary leader for the witches? Absolutely.

'Just let her pass or fail on her own merit,' I replied firmly. 'I think she'll be an asset, but don't do anything to her application on my account. Nepotism and bribes have already ruined the Council. If we want to build it again from the ground up, we need to do it right. No one buys their way in, no one bribes their way in, and if anyone approaches anyone about doing either of those things, they are to report it to me. Clear?' And then I'd sic Bastion on them.

Kass grinned, 'Clear. I knew you'd say that but the others made me ask. I'll feed it back. Now, why are we all being gathered here? It feels like a murder mystery. If Bastion starts killing us, I'll shove Shirdal in front of me and run.'

I laughed. 'You're safe. Come on. Follow me to the kitchen where the others are.'

Chapter 60

I led Kass into the kitchen where the others were milling about. Shirdal and Reynard flew to each other like metal to a magnet. Profanities were uttered and then the two men were kissing, a tangle of limbs shoved hard against my kitchen wall, knocking into my brand-new mug shelf.

'Hey!' I called. 'If you break a mug, you have to buy me an exact replica of it! They have sentimental value!'

'Who's the dark-winged one?' Mum asked in a loud stage whisper.

'Reynard,' Oscar explained. 'One of the Dark Seraph, bound to Emory as brethren. It caused a bit of a stir.' At times, he was king of the understatement. The look that Jinx shot him suggested she agreed with my assessment.

'No politics!' Emory interjected. He cleared his throat. 'Shirdal, Reynard – you want to get a room?'

Reluctantly the two men pulled apart but Shirdal didn't take his eyes off Reynard as he replied, 'We are able to control ourselves.' He grinned as he added a muttered, 'For now anyway, my Azhdar.' He laced his fingers through Reynard's then turned back to us.

That was when he noticed the ring on my finger. A genuine beam lit across his face. '*Bah bah doostam!*' he clapped Bastion on his shoulder. '*Mobârake!*'

Bastion bowed a little. 'Thank you, *rahbar*.'

Shirdal let go of Reynard and pulled me into a hug. 'Congratulations, Amber. I do not need to tell you of the worth of the man you are marrying.'

I smiled. 'No, you do not.'

He grinned at me and lightly rapped his knuckles against my head. 'Took you long enough,' he teased.

'In fairness, he didn't make it easy.'

'Nothing easy is worth working for.' Shirdal grinned. 'This calls for rum! Where is the rum?' He started rummaging in our kitchen cupboards.

I held up my hand to our assembled friends and family. 'We're engaged,' I announced happily, even though the announcement was now somewhat otiose. My mum let out a happy noise reminiscent of the shriek Jinx had given on my doorstep. Oscar hugged Bastion, whilst Mum hugged me, then Bastion and I swapped hug partners. I saw Mum murmur something to Bastion, making him pale slightly.

Oscar hugged me tightly. 'Wonderful news,' he murmured gruffly.

'I expect you to follow suit,' I whispered back. Oscar winked, making my heart swell. 'There's no time like the present,' I prodded.

We both knew that more than so many others. For so long, Mum had been lost to us – present and alive, but not the woman we knew or needed. It was a miracle that she was back, a miracle I would never take for granted. There were still some conversations to be had, like discussing her choice to hide my familiar from me and get my mind cleared, but we had time now for those words.

I had no doubt that Mum's application to the council would pass because she was a formidable witch, one I was looking forward to seeing in action.

'This is your day,' Oscar replied. 'I wouldn't steal your thunder for anything. But soon.'

I grinned. Bastion and I had said 'soon' and he'd proposed the next day. I wondered how long Oscar would be able to hold off.

Shirdal was mixing rum and Cokes whilst Reynard balanced little cocktail umbrellas on the glasses and handed them out. Emory and Jinx were animatedly telling a story which, judging by Benji's guffaws, was hilarious. Frogmatch was under the table, surreptitiously making shoelace art out of Jinx's boots. Charlize – my stepdaughter-to-be – was laughing with Mum about something.

Warm arms encircled me. 'I love you, witch,' Bastion whispered into the shell of my ear, making a delicious shudder run through me.

'I love you too, griffin.' I turned my head to kiss one of the hard biceps curled around me. 'What did my mum say to you?' I asked curiously.

'She said that if I ever hurt you she would kill me and destroy any evidence that I ever lived.'

'Nice.'

He grinned. 'Don't tell anyone, but she's about the only person that's ever scared me.'

I laughed. 'Your secret's safe with me.' I turned to face him. 'Thank you.'

'For what?'

'For everything. It's perfect.'

He lowered his lips to my ear, 'You can make it up to me later. I thought we could play "sexy librarian and overdue-book-returner".'

I studied the man I loved, 'In this scenario ... you're the sexy librarian, aren't you?'

He smirked. 'I've got some glasses especially.'

I imagined him wearing a pair of glasses on his nose and nothing else other than a frown at me for returning a book late... I bit my lip. The temperature in the room seemed to rise a handful of degrees.

His lips curled up. 'I knew you'd like that one. I've been saving it for a special occasion and I think this qualifies, don't you?'

'It does,' I agreed briskly, like I wasn't a puddle of desire. 'That sounds like an excellent plan.' I cleared my throat awkwardly; I was the worst at sexy talk.

'Good. Pick the book that's going to be overdue. You'll be reading passages from it ... so pick a *good* one.'

I was tempted for half a second to choose the dictionary or something equally dry, but the thought of reading some sections of my racier romance books to him had me discarding that particular idea.

Bastion released me with a quick kiss then began circulating among our guests, as if he hadn't just been whispering dirty plans for later in my ear.

My husband-to-be was sexy as sin, and I was grateful to the Goddess that he was mine. Now that I'd found him, I was keeping him forever – and woe betide anyone who tried to tear us asunder. Our future lay before us and I had no doubt that at times it would be difficult, but with Bastion by my side, there was nothing we couldn't accomplish. My heart was full and I was happy in a way I'd never been in my entire life. I had friends, family and a position I was proud of. I had already accomplished so much, and it was only just the beginning.

I was ready to face anything that was coming. Bring it on.

I hope you've loved Amber and Bastion as much as I have. They have been an absolute blast to write. If you're not ready to let them go yet, grab yourself an extra scene

from Bastion's POV here: https://BookHip.com/ZSJZ
WBP

What's Next?

If you're hankering after some more tales in the Other realm, have you read Jinx's books? My level-headed PI who discovers magic? Head on over to book 1 in that series, *Glimmer of the Other*. Or perhaps try Lucy's tale? My fish-out-of-water accountant turned alpha were-wolf. Grab book 1, *Protection of the Pack*.

Talking of Lucy... a brand new instalment in her series, Awakening the Pack, will be coming in 2024. Link to pre-order here.

If you've already read everything in the Other realm, then why not try my brand new world, written with Jilleen Dolbeare? Start with *The Vampire and the Case of her Dastardly Death.*

I awoke dead. It was a real bummer. Being covered in blood and having fangs was the icing on an already terrible day.

Book 2, *The Vampire and the case of the Wayward Werewolf is coming 1st March 2024. Pre-order here.*

I hope you've enjoyed Amber and Bastion as much as I have. They have found a forever place in my heart!

If you'd like some FREE BOOKS then join my newsletter and you can get a couple of free stories, as well as pictures of my dog and other helpful things.

Patreon

I have started my very own Patreon page. What is Patreon? It's a subscription service that allows you to support me AND read my books way before anyone else! For a small monthly fee you could be reading my next book, on a weekly chapter-by-chapter basis (in its roughest draft form!) in the next week or two. If you hit "Join the community" you can follow me along for free, though you won't get access to all the good stuff, like early release books, polls, live Q&A's, character art and more! You can even have a video call with me or have a character named after you! My current patrons are getting to read a novella called House Bound which isn't available anywhere else, not even to my newsletter subscribers!

If you're too impatient to wait until my next release, then Patreon is made for you! Join my patrons here.

My Online Store

One final note, I am now selling audiobooks and merchandise direct from my store. Have a snoop at https://shop.heathergharris.com/ There are hoodies, t-shirts, candles and stickers and all sorts of glorious things to discover. Buying audiobooks directly from me is the best way to support me, but if you're set in your ways, then never fear! The new audiobooks will be widely available soon.

Other Works by Heather

The *Other Realm* Series

Book .5 Glimmer of Dragons (a prequel story),

Book 1 Glimmer of The Other,

Book 2 Glimmer of Hope,

Book 2.5 Glimmer of Christmas (a Christmas tale),

Book 3 Glimmer of Death,

Book 4 Glimmer of Deception,

Book 5 Challenge of the Court,

Book 6 Betrayal of the Court; and

Book 7 Revival of the Court.

The *Other Wolf* Series

Book .5 Defender of The Pack(a prequel story),

Book 1 Protection of the Pack,

Book 2 Guardians of the Pack,

Book 3 Saviour of The Pack, and

Book 4 Awakening of The Pack.

The *Other Witch* Series

Book .5 Rune of the Witch(a prequel story),

Book 1 Hex of the Witch,

Book 2 Coven of the Witch;,

Book 3 Familiar of the Witch, and

Book 4 Destiny of the Witch.

The *Portlock Paranormal Detective* Series with Jilleen Dolbeare

Book .5 The Vampire and the case of her Dastardly Death,

Book 1 The Vampire and the case of the Wayward Werewolf,(coming March 2024)

About Heather

Heather is an urban fantasy writer and mum. She was born and raised near Windsor, which gave her the misguided impression that she was close to royalty in some way. She is not, though she once got a letter from Queen Elizabeth II's lady-in-waiting.

Heather went to university in Liverpool, where she took up skydiving and met her future husband. When she's not running around after her children, she's plotting her next book and daydreaming about vampires, dragons and kick-ass heroines.

Heather is a book lover who grew up reading Brian Jacques and Anne McCaffrey. She loves to travel and once spent a month in Thailand. She vows to return.

Want to learn more about Heather? Subscribe to her newsletter for behind-the-scenes scoops, free bonus material and a cheeky peek into her world. Her subscribers will always get the heads up about the best deals on her books.

Subscribe to her Newsletter at her website www.heatherg harris.com/subscribe.

Too impatient to wait for Heather's next book? Join her (ever growing!) army of supportive patrons at Patreon.

Heather's Patreon

Heather has started her very own Patreon page. What is Patreon? It's a subscription service that allows you to support Heather AND read her books way before anyone else! For a small monthly fee you could be reading Heather's next book, on a weekly chapter-by-chapter basis (in its roughest draft form!) in the next week or two. If you hit "Join the community" you can follow Heather along for FREE, though you won't get access to all the good stuff, like early release books, polls, live Q&A's, character art and more! You can even have a video call with Heather or have a character named after you! Heather's current patrons are getting to read a novella called House Bound which isn't available anywhere else, not even to her newsletter subscribers!

If you're too impatient to wait until Heather's next release, then Patreon is made for you! Join Heather's patrons.

Heather's Shop

Heather has created a glorious online shop. There you can buy oodles of glorious merchandise and audiobooks directly from her. Heather's audiobooks will still be on sale elsewhere, of course, but Heather pays her audiobook narrator *and* her cover designer - she makes the entire product - and then certain providers pays her 25% per sale. OUCH. Where possible, Heather would love it if you could buy her audiobooks directly from her, and then she can keep an amazing 90% of the money instead. Which she can use to reinvest in more books, in every form!

But Audiobooks isn't all there is in the shop. You can get hoodies, t-shirts, stickers, mugs and more! Go and check her store out at: https://shop.heathergharris.com/

Stay in Touch

Heather has been working hard on a bunch of cool things, including a website which you'll love. Check it out at w ww.heathergharris.com.

Contact Info: www.heathergharris.com
Email: HeatherGHarrisAuthor@gmail.com

Social Media

Heather can also be found on a host of social medias:

Facebook Page

Facebook Reader Group

Goodreads

Bookbub

Instagram

If you get a chance, please do follow Heather on Amazon!

Reviews

Reviews feed Heather's soul. She'd really appreciate it if you could take a few moments to review her books on Amazon,
Bookbub, or Goodreads and say hello.

Made in United States
Troutdale, OR
03/27/2024

18719659R00212